GIVEN

STAR BREED: BOOK ONE

ELIN WYN

CLOCK
WALK
PUBLISHING

KARA

*I*t was all Juda's fault.

I kicked him out of my bed three weeks ago for cheating on me, but apparently, he wasn't done screwing me over.

I crouched low on the roof of the abandoned gambling den across the street from Sary's "general store" and cursed the limp-dicked bastard all over again.

There wasn't a lot of traffic at this time of day. Not that that meant much in Ghelfi; the thieves' city never truly slept. There was no point in waiting for night, like in the old vids Mom used to watch over and over. Like all sealed cities on the surface of Neurea, lighting in Ghelfi varied throughout the day's cycle, but never to a true night.

I saw real night, once. I stowed away on the back of a surface crawler that was heading to Lashell. I don't know why, somehow I'd thought it would be better if I got out of Ghelfi, started over somewhere else.

The velvet sky, studded with stars, shone clean and cold. Perfect. Not like the barely organized chaos of the cities.

But halfway there, the crawler broke down, had to be towed back. I realized then that there was no way out. Not for me.

1

In the old vids, everything always turned out alright, something swooped in at the last minute to save the day.

That's how you knew they were only lies.

So here I was, half-hidden among old wires and debris that had been kicked up to the top of the store years ago, long forgotten. Watching time slip away on the chrono, crossing my fingers to old gods I didn't believe in.

"What'cha doing?"

I jumped, furious with myself.

Bani crouched next to me. His dark brown hair hung down in his face, but I could still see the twinkle in his eye. Snuck up on me and was proud of it, little bastard.

I socked him gently in the arm, just enough to let him know I cared.

"Everybody's looking for you, Kara," he said under his breath. He didn't look at me but instead kept his eyes scanning across the street, trying to see what I was interested in. Smart kid.

I ran my hand through my own tangle of hair. It was past time to cut it, but things had been a little busy lately.

"How mad is Xavis?" I really didn't want to know the answer.

Bani shrugged one bony shoulder. "He's playing it down a little bit, but I think he's pretty steamed. If you, of all people, don't show up by the end of the tithe, he's gonna lose a lot of face."

A light crackled, the burnt smell of frying wires wafted by. But I wasn't paying attention to the noise or to the stink of ozone that permeated the air of Ghelfi. If Xavis really was mad, I was in trouble.

I shoved the thought far to the back of my head. Nothing to do about it but keep moving.

A shuffling sound below surprised me, and I risked another glance over the ledge. A miner, wrapped in rags so filthy there was no telling the gender, half-staggered down the street. He, she, whatever, paused in front of Sary's storefront, then stumbled inside.

Ice gripped my spine. Rings willing, he'd be quick. Claim whatever he came to trade, and get out. Not stay there, spinning stories of life in the Waste, screwing my timetable.

"Is that the job?" Bani's wide eyes fixed me. "A snatch and grab on the miners after they bring in the dust?"

I rolled my eyes. "They're just trying to get by, same as us." Besides, credits were no good to me, not with so little time to clean them. But the antonium dust the miners brought in was untraceable. 'Dust knows no provenance' was the saying. I just needed to get enough of it.

Agonizing minutes passed until he left. I glanced at my chrono again. If she didn't show up today, I didn't have a backup plan. This was my backup plan. No more nets to catch my fall.

I closed my eyes to try to find the calm, cold center within that had kept me alive so far on the streets of Ghelfi, and waited. I didn't need to see, didn't need to check the time. I could only wait and listen.

Finally, the sound came. The sharp click of stiletto heels across the permasteel walkway. I opened my eyes and leaned forward ever so slightly to peer down the street.

There she was. Charro's secret indulgence. Silver hair teased into a high fall down her back, her face paint marked her as one of Sary's working girls. When I first found out about Charro's extracurricular activities, I'd half thought of sending a note to Sary, stir up the nest a bit. Then I started thinking long term. That'd been almost two years ago.

Two years of planning and waiting brought to a crash by that bastard Juda. I should have gutted him like a fish instead of just kicking him out.

Bani glanced at her and then looked up at me, frowning.

"That's your mark?" He risked another look but I pulled him back sharply by the collar of his jacket.

He glared at me, with all the scorn a preteen could manage. "I know her. She works the landing pad. Even if she did have the sort of money you're going to need to get out of trouble with Xavis, she isn't gonna be carrying it with her on a job." His eyes narrowed. "So what are you really up to?"

I grinned. I couldn't help it. I wasn't pleased to have to use this job to get out of the hole Juda left me in, but it was pretty brilliant.

"Just keep your eye on the alley, kid, okay?"

I checked my chrono again, but I didn't need to. I'd timed this pattern so often. Like clockwork, the shadows of Charro's two goons came into focus on the tinted plex of the storefront. Just like every other time I'd watched, they paced back and forth, no doubt joking about their boss and his hobby.

"They're supposed to be guarding the back room, but he always kicks them out when she visits." I checked the time again, stupid habit. Couldn't help it. "He might be there, but he's more than a little distracted right now."

I worked my way across the roof, down to the collection of rubble in the back alley that had let me gain my vantage point.

Bani followed me and I glared at him.

"Stay up here," I snarled. "I don't know how this is going to turn out."

"Then you'll need a second pair of hands."

The kid had a point, but I'd be damned if I was going to let him have it.

"No, I need a second pair of eyes." His shoulders sagged a little. But I couldn't be sure he wouldn't follow me anyway.

"Besides, I don't know if I can trust you on this job." His white face told me my words hit their mark. Hated to do it, but I didn't want to be worried about him. I was in enough trouble as it was.

His face slid out of sight as I worked my way down the trash heap.

Even before I crossed the street, the bitter stench of the acid bombs I'd planted clawed at my throat. The air recirculators only worked intermittently in this neighborhood, and in the alley, the smell almost forced me to my knees.

That the miner walked by without flinching, I could understand. I'd heard too much time in an environmental suit would have you smelling nothing but rubber. But the silver-haired doxy must have been high on something to not notice something was wrong.

No time to linger in the alley. Microcams swept every ninety seconds, watching, waiting for anything out of the ordinary.

I dashed to the hiding space I'd carved out of the fallen wall that backed up to Sary's, and held my breath, trying to hear over the drumming of my heartbeat. The rushing in my ears slowed, and I poked my head out. Still all clear.

Nobody in their right mind would take on Sary, he ran half the games in town, and word in the pits said he wanted to take control of the city over from Xavis. Unlikely, but still, not someone I really wanted after me. But if the choice was Sary or Xavis himself….well, it was a sucky choice.

I counted, waiting for the next clear moment to check on the results of the clustered acid bombs, then ran back around the corner.

Ninety seconds is a long time.

Ninety seconds is long enough to make one chip in the wall a day until a section can be lifted away and replaced seamlessly.

Ninety seconds is long enough to plant one small acid bomb at a time, then wait for a few days for the smell to dissipate, for the interior wall that led to the vault to weaken, bit by bit, day by day.

Ninety seconds is long enough to die in the Waste, outside of the protection of the domes.

And if I didn't get my tithe to Xavis by tonight, that's where I'd end up.

DAVIEN

*R*eally, everything would be so much easier if I just snapped the fat fool's neck. Only the endless lessons in control back on the ship kept my hands still at my sides, fingers barely flexing. The tips of my claws ran across my palms, bringing me back to focus.

"Davien, are you even listening to me?" Xavis rumbled.

And he wasn't a fool, even if I despised him. Xavis had clawed his way to the top of the dirtiest pile to run Ghelfi. The trip to the top had been over the broken bodies of plenty of enemies. He'd stayed on his perch for over twenty Imperial years. I didn't have to do much research to know his methods hadn't changed.

Prime example: he'd hired me.

I focused on Xavis, only too aware I'd started to slip away into the hunt. Every moment here, stuck on this rock, was a delay I couldn't afford. Xavis, bastard though he might be, was my fastest way out of here. Well, the fastest way without an unacceptably high casualty count.

Xavis lounged in his hover chair, fingers tapping in annoyance well away from the control pad. The chair was as much affectation as convenience - he could walk just fine. Just liked to be able to loom over people.

"She's late," he growled. "She's never late."

I didn't need to ask who he meant. He'd been on a tear about his precious Kara for hours, first calling her his brightest find, then cursing her ingratitude.

The large room I'd come to think of as the receiving hall was mostly empty now, just the regular workers at their terminals around the edges, cleaning credits, shifting funds until they could be transferred into the most secure banks in the Empire. Repetitive, mind-numbing, but crucial to any modern criminal enterprise. The low drone as they worked filled the otherwise quiet room.

The last traces of the dark festivities of the last day had almost been erased. All day and night long, denizens of Ghelfi's underworld had streamed in, bringing their tribute to the acknowledged boss of the city, doing their best, or worst, to please a capricious overlord. The whole affair had been boring, and stupidly inefficient.

But the archaic ritual soothed his ego and had been an opening to a job. At the last tithing, some idiot with more guts than brains had tried to take Xavis out. He'd failed to account for the force shield over the hover chair, but his explosives did thin out Xavis' bodyguards considerably.

Bad luck for them, perfect timing for me. When Doc had commanded we all enter the escape pods, she'd made it clear we were to jump as randomly as possible. It should have worked, should have drawn the attackers away from the *Daedalus*, but it had been six standard weeks since I'd crashed here, and I hadn't had a signal from her or any of my brothers.

If I was on my own, I needed credits. And I needed a lot of them.

Six weeks had been enough to battle my way up the ranks of

Xavis' enforcers. Not that they were slouches, but they didn't have my, shall we say, advantages.

A commotion at the entrance to the room drew my attention, and I angled for a better position at the front of Xavis's chair. The dais we stood on served as an excellent vantage point for the room, allowing me to take in any suspicious movements at a glance. I'd argued to get rid of the scarlet drapery behind us, observing it provided too obvious of a hiding place. He'd refused. Like the dais, it was all about show.

The scuffle at the doorway turned out to be two enforcers dragging a third man between them. Beneath the new scrapes and swelling around his eye, I recognized him. Marcus, Martin, something like that. A low-level hustler who worked the dive bars near the station. Rigged games of chance, targeting travelers who wouldn't be around long enough to make a fuss.

Xavis waved me back into place, and I relaxed, just a tad. This wasn't a threat to his authority, just another loser trapped here.

The enforcers tossed the poor sap onto the lowest level of the dais and stepped back, waiting for orders.

"Malik," Xavis coaxed the hover chair to the edge of the dais, watching the human wreck below take shuddering breaths. "You didn't appear for the tithing last night." He floated down, a pale mass of malevolence, eyes narrowed.

I stepped behind him. I didn't expect trouble from Malik, but there'd be hell to pay if I wasn't where Xavis expected me, especially when he was in this mood.

"Well?" Xavis's low voice was almost pleasant, but a thread of malice wound through it, unmistakable. "We've known each other for so long, I'm surprised that you've disappointed me."

"I'm sorry, Lord Xavis," the man mumbled. Probably had lost a few teeth. "My youngest has been down with the Batdu pox, the medicine was so much…" He gulped. "I thought I could make it up before the tithing."

"Oh?" Xavis's eyes glittered. "How is the poor thing doing now?"

"Better now, Lord Xavis. Thank you."

"You should have told me, I would have lent you the money."

Sure he would have. At rates that would mean he'd own the service of the entire family.

"But, as it is, we have a problem that needs to be sorted out." Xavis made a show of tapping his fingers, as if considering, but that sharp brain had already decided on the punishment, I was sure. This was just to terrorize the hustler, and send a message to everyone else in the room.

"I'd forgotten about your lovely family," he purred. "The oldest is twelve now, as I recall?"

The man shifted uneasily. "Yes, my lord. But she's not very strong…"

"I'm sure a more active life will be good for her. She'll have her own tithe to pay, starting next cycle."

"What?" The man pushed himself to his feet, protesting.

Idiot.

Xavis flicked a finger, and I sprang to the front of the chair to grab the beaten hustler by the front of his jacket. I lifted him off the floor and shook him until his head snapped back.

He pushed feebly against my grip.

"I wouldn't try it," I growled, and he froze.

I'm not sure what it is about my voice. On the ship, with my brothers, no one had a problem with it. In all the training vids we watched, I never thought I sounded that different. But here, on this worthless rock at the fringe of the Empire, all I had to do was speak, and the humans cowered.

Weak.

Prey.

I snarled, and the acrid scent of urine assaulted me. The fucker had wet himself. Apparently, he hadn't liked the points of my teeth, either.

"I suggest you comply, little man. What choice do you have?"

He stared at me, face pale beneath the marks of the beating, but finally nodded. It wasn't much of a motivational speech, but it was the truth. No one on Neurea had a lot of choices.

"I think you can release him now, Davien." The smug tone of Xavis's voice told me he'd gotten what he wanted. He hadn't had to send a usually reliable worker to the Wastes, and he'd picked up extra leverage at the same time.

I lowered the man back to his feet. His legs buckled, but he scrambled away from me on hands and knees. Idiot. I wasn't the worst monster in the room.

The rest of the negotiations were predictably short and one-sided. The hustler left, and the business in the room resumed its quiet drone.

"I've decided." Xavis's voice cracked like a whip as he floated back to the top of the dais. "An example must be made."

I waited below for orders.

"Find Kara Shimshi. Bring her to me."

Despite my better instincts, I grinned.

The hunt was on.

KARA

I waited, checking my chrono obsessively, preparing the last items, until the first moment the microcams flew away. The way was clear, but not for long.

Ninety.

The false covering of the weakened wall came off easily. I set it on the ground next to me, hands shaking.

Any loud, unexpected sound in the area would summon the microcams out of their regular routine, and my ninety seconds would be over fast.

Ideally, I would have waited days after the last of my corrosive little beasties had done their work. That would have been plenty of time for the area to be safe. But now I'd have to work the job despite a dulled sense of touch through an acid-proof glove.

One tentative push through the jagged opening, another against the half-dissolved back wall of the safe.

Eighty.

A final push, and nothing but empty space beyond. I was in.

The opening was narrow, barely wide enough to slide my hand through, but there was no time to widen it. Now that I'd breached their security, there'd never be an opening like this again.

Even through the glove, I could feel the triangular prism shape of the antonium vials. I grabbed one and, slower than I would've liked, eased it out to place in the pouch I'd unfolded while waiting.

Each vial would nestle in a separate pocket. Antonium had a reputation for nasty surprises when jostled about.

Sweat ran down my back, measuring the seconds in fear. I'd wipe it off later. No time now.

Eyes watering from the fumes that still lingered in the alley-way, I reached through the gap for another vial, then another.

Seventy.

The urge to just grab a handful, stuff them in my pack and be gone shook my chest. But the hole wasn't large enough for a fisted hand. I had to wrap my fingers underneath each prism and slowly coax it out towards me.

Another one nestled in its pocket.

The sting of the acid against the flesh of my arm began to burn. I hadn't thought it would still be so potent when I came in for the job, I'd assumed the gloves would be enough. I reached for another vial. Better some scars on my arm than to be tossed into the Waste.

Fifty.

"My hands are smaller, let me do it."

Crap. "What are you doing here?" I hissed between my teeth, trying not to split my attention, and knowing I was failing.

"I want to help," Bani whispered back. "Here, I can..." As he reached towards the opening, his foot caught the edge of the section of wall I'd removed.

The sheet of permasteel wobbled once, twice, and then fell with a clatter that could be heard for blocks. The shrill whir of the microcams changing direction, picking up speed, told me in no uncertain terms we'd been noticed.

I snatched my hand back from the opening. One last vial, no time to gently pack it. The long strap of the bag went over my head, and I grabbed Bani.

"I'm sorry..." he started.

"Just run," was all I had time to say.

"You there, wait!" The heavy footfalls of the goons as they emerged from the shop punctuated the sound of the microcams.

The chase was on.

I grinned. I couldn't help it. I'd been running through the streets and alleys of Ghelfi for over half my life. The hit of adrenaline, the intense focus on the next step, the next jump, left no room for any other worries.

In the alley behind the row of gambling dens that all paid tithe to Xavis, we could hear the murmur of winners and losers, a soft rush of voices that faded as we darted down another small passageway, twisting and turning. But still, the cams were on us. The goons didn't need to be fast, just keep their tracking on.

The smell of fried noodles hit me; we were behind Artin's place. He'd always looked the other way when I snagged leftover food from the trash as a kid. My stomach growled, heedless of the current crisis.

If we got out of this, if I survived the tithe, I'd treat Bani to a feast.

If.

Into the oldest section of Ghelfi city, alleys filled with broken parts not even worth the recycle bounty, snarled nests of wires cracking between buildings, dodging the dangling streamers, because you never knew what was still live and what could kill you.

"Kara," Bani gasped from behind me. "I can't keep up." His voice broke, sobbing for air as we ran.

"Just a bit farther, I promise." I hated promising. I hate lying and promises too often end up that way, at least in our world. But if we could just make it a few blocks further, we had a chance.

Legs aching, we sprinted across the street of the main bazaar, dodging the tramline filled with tourists and miners and gamblers and suckers that all thought that here, on the fringe of the Empire, they'd make their dreams come true.

"Through here," I called over my shoulder, and darted between two dingy storefronts, back in the shelter of the alleys.

On the streets, it was too easy for a goon or a drone to take a shot. Needlers were illegal in the Empire, which meant everyone seemed to have at least a pair on Neurea as a badge of citizenship. Everyone except me. Needlers, pretty much all guns, made me queasy. Not for the first time, I wondered if I should re-evaluate that plan.

The back ways, left over from when the huge assembler machines had formed the basic structures of the city back in the day, zigged and zagged in a tangled pattern. Their creators probably thought it made perfect sense, but they were all long dead.

Finally, the maintenance shaft I'd been homing in on came within sight. My fingers laced in the grill, jerking it off as I skidded to a stop.

"Told you..." I was talking to the air. Bani was gone.

Rings. I needed to get away, get clear of the area and to Xavis and get shit straightened out. It wasn't my fault the stupid kid tagged along. Hell, it was his fault we were running now.

Damn it.

I stashed the bag in the shaft. No point risking it, even if I was an idiot.

I headed back the way we'd come, slower this time. If Bani had just gotten lost, that would be one thing... but if he'd been caught, I didn't feel like rushing my head into a noose.

"Get your hands off me, you jerk!" The yelling made a great beacon and a warning. I poked my head around the corner and pulled back right away. They'd caught him, the darker haired of the goons holding Bani's thin frame pressed against the wall of the old water plant, seepage running out from under the wall, turning the dust underfoot to mud.

The kid kicked in his grip, but he'd need to weigh at least four times as much to make any difference. I risked another look, discarding options as fast as I came up with them. A crackle overhead caught my attention. Maybe….

Digging through the rubbish, I found a length of scrap wire. I pulled out my knife and started wrapping it.

It wasn't a great plan, but it was all I had. I eased out from the corner and waved. Bani saw me, and I pointed overhead, then to the ledge of a boarded up window next to him. His eyes widened, but he nodded.

Then he bit the hell out of the arm of the goon holding him.

Bastard hadn't expected that, and he dropped Bani. Instead of falling like a rock, Bani wiggled, twisting his body so he caught the edge of the windowsill with the tips of his fingers.

"Don't fall, kid," I muttered, and threw my knife into the tangle of wires overhead.

For a long moment, it looked like my gamble had failed. The knife tangled in the cluster above, the long wire I'd wrapped around the blade trailing into the damp dirt below. But nothing was happening. Then, with a shriek of metal on metal, the whole tangled mess tumbled down, catching the goons and the bots in their net.

Both thugs lay in the damp ground, twitching slightly. It didn't look like the shock had been enough to kill them, even if the electronics were fried. One small knot untangled in my gut. I'd made it so far without killing anyone, at least that I knew about.

Movement on the wall caught my attention. Bani still clung there, pressed tight against the wall. I guess, if that was my choice today, I could live with it.

Bani worked his way hand over hand down the windowsill towards me and dropped to the ground, well clear of the danger zone. He looked up at me, grinning. "That was great."

I ran my hand through my hair and smothered the urge to shake him. "Belay that. The cams probably got our faces, probably sent them to the servers. The trouble isn't over."

My hand drifted to my side, fingers ghosting over the sheath. "And I've lost my favorite knife."

His face fell. "Thanks for coming back for me," he whispered.

I punched his arm. "Of course, idiot." Maybe I should have hugged him. But that would have been weird for both of us.

He must have known what I meant, because he perked right back up, nearly skipping in circles around me as we headed back to the hiding place. "Did you get enough to make tithe? Maybe extra to sweeten Xavis back up? He's only angry because he likes you, you know."

At his age, the tithe would be pretty minimal. It was for most kids, made it easy to agree, trade a little of the take for protection, for food. For the semblance of a family, when you had no one else.

Xavis had always pushed me harder, said I had a talent for the game that would be a shame not to develop. Unfortunately, his idea of encouragement was to push, and push hard.

My tithes had always been twice the other kids' in our band of castaways and orphans.

But still, it was better than starving.

I'd pulled eight vials out from the safe before Bani had shown up to 'help.' "It'll be enough, maybe even a little left over as a buffer." For all the chaos, even with having to push the timeline on the plan, it had worked. Xavis would forgive me being late with such a haul. The vise around my chest finally started to loosen. It was gonna be alright.

"After I check in, let's go hit up old Artin's place, get some station-style noodles?"

Bani nodded and started chattering about all the other fabulous treats in the street stands on the way. I half listened to him, half paid attention to the noise of the bazaar, the smells and sounds from all over the System. Things were going to work out. I could find a new long-term job, something that would really...

We turned the final corner back to the maintenance shaft and froze. Shock flipped a switch, filling my veins with fire.

"Hey!" I shouted. "Get away from that!"

A black-uniformed man hunched over my hiding place. The grill had been tossed into the alley and he crouched, head bowed down, peering into the shaft. He didn't flinch. I reached for my knife and swore at the empty sheath.

Instead, I grabbed a cracked tile, discarded years ago, and flung it at the guy. A rushing noise filled my ears, drowning out the city, Bani, everything. I'd gone through way too much hassle to lose the haul to a scavenger like that.

Except this wasn't like any scavenger I'd ever seen. Too neat, too clean. I would have thought he was military, if the Empire ever bothered to send anyone this far out.

The invader might have ignored my shouts, but the edge of the tile cracked against his shoulder. There was something wrong with his movements as the black form slowly rose and turned my way.

His face was covered by a dark helmet, but all my attention was focused on the satchel in his hand. My satchel. My vials. My only hope.

"Get away!" I shrieked and tore towards him. I might not have my knife, but you didn't survive in Ghelfi City without learning a few things about a street fight. He might have been bigger than me, but I could count on desperation to lend me extra strength.

This day just wasn't going to stop, was it? I had to have that satchel. I flung myself at the dark shape, snatching the loop of the bag as I went by.

My own momentum snapped me back. The black-uniformed presence didn't move, didn't speak. I rushed at him, hoping to knock him over, get him to loosen his grip on my satchel.

Nothing. He stood as immovable as the rocks outside in the Waste. I grabbed another tile, ignoring the sting of the sharp edge that cut my hands, and smashed my fist with its improvised blade against the black helmet.

Didn't even scratch it. What the hell was this thing? I made another snatch at the satchel, pulling until the muscles in my arms screamed.

Suddenly, the motionless figure snapped. He twisted, shaking me like a toy at the end of the string, until one final flip sent me flying into the opposite wall. Someone dropped a pile of permasteel bricks on my head, and blackness took me.

DAVIEN

The stink of fear and worry flashed through the room as Xavis pulled up a holo of the girl from his control chair. Nothing special to look at, shoulder length dark hair, copper skin, slight frame. The pose of the image looked wary, as if she were always braced for a blow.

"There's not a height reference," I muttered. "Would be helpful."

Xavis flicked his eyes at me. Apparently, he still hadn't figured out I wasn't like the rest of his lackeys, too afraid to ask for the basic information needed to get the job done efficiently.

"You!" he snapped. "Monitor 27. Stand up and turn around."

Silence fell across the hall as a woman rose, shaking, from one of the workstations on the left wall.

"She's about the same height," Xavis answered, but his eyes were on the holo.

Not a single keyboard click could be heard as I approached the woman. Her eyes darted from side to side, searching for an escape, help, anything. She wouldn't find it here, in the depths of Xavis' lair.

But I didn't need to make this worse for her. "You and you," I gestured to the men who had been working at stations on either side. "Stand up."

They obeyed, and if they took the chance to step a little closer to the terrified woman, I didn't think less of them for it. A futile effort, if I'd meant to attack her, but they fought against their fear.

And it made it easier to judge her height against theirs, giving me a better measurement for Kara.

"That's enough," I waved at them and turned my back.

I stalked out of the reception hall, conscious of the weight of all those eyes boring into me. It wasn't a matter for concern; it'd been clear for weeks that no one would challenge me.

Outside the hall, I eyed the lift tube. Xavis' reception hall was at the deepest level of his complex. It would be faster by far to take the tube to the surface level and then start my search for his missing thief.

But I hated the enclosed space, the stink of fear and despair soaked into the walls of the lift tube scraped my nerves raw every time I stepped inside.

Decision made, I pivoted and palmed open the panel that led to the stairwell. It shouldn't have taken much longer to walk up the stairs, except on every landing clusters of children huddled.

Too young still to be sent out to work, orphaned kids or the offspring of Xavis' bound servants, they hid throughout the complex, keeping each other quiet.

As usual, I stepped around them quickly. One level up, and another, and halfway there. I fixed the image of Kara in my mind. Ghelfi City wasn't large, but with the maze of old streets and rundown buildings, she could be anywhere. Xavis had given me a short list of her possible contacts, but, to be honest, I wouldn't mind a nice long hunt.

A thin scream broke my musing, and I spun, back to the wall, eyes searching for the source of the sound. At the top of the next flight of stairs, a small child wavered unsteadily, outstretched arms flailing. A slightly older boy reached for her, but only brushed her fingertips as she fell backward, head aiming for the sharp edge of the steps below.

Dammit.

I leaped up the stairs, dodging the other children pressed against the wall. Just a second more... My left hand barely had room to slide between her dark curls and the ceramasteel before I tucked her against my torso and twisted, taking the impact on my side.

She squirmed in my arms, and I loosed my grip on her. Tiny, bones as fragile as a bird, sharp planes stood out on cheeks that should have been plump. No room for childhood here. Her eyes were wide as she pushed up, to sit straddling my chest.

"Can you catch me again?"

I blinked. It's a point of pride for me to never be surprised, but that was unexpected.

"Well, if you fall again..." I started.

She leaned forward, reaching past my face to brush my hair back. "Your ears are pointy!" She started to play with the tip of my left ear when I carefully guided her arm away.

"It's not polite to play with other people's faces," I growled.

A flash of blue-clad arms and her tiny frame was whisked away. "What are you doing here," a low voice snapped.

I stood up slowly, stretching to my full height, looking over the new actor on the scene. A young man, barely older than the kids clustered around him, stood on the landing above me. He passed the girl to another child behind him without breaking eye contact with me.

Points to him. Tougher than most of the adults in this town, if not necessarily brighter.

"Just keeping her head from cracking," I answered, and started moving up the stairs, towards the crowd gathered at the landing. "And now I'm on my way."

"It's true, Hoyt," one of the boys chimed in. "She fell, and he caught her."

ELIN WYN

The young man, Hoyt, didn't look convinced, but it didn't really matter.

"You're not wanted here," he snarled.

"Cub, if you can keep me out, feel free." I passed him on the landing and continued my climb. "Otherwise, I have things to do." Halfway to the next landing, I glanced behind me to meet his glare. "And if you're in charge, take better care of your wards."

The curly haired moppet squirmed out from her keeper's arms to wave at me. "Bye, mister!"

I waved back, and pulled my mind back to the hunt at hand. Part of me recoiled at the thought of how badly, how inefficiently the city was run. Thought about how thin the girl was, how thin and dirty they all were. The fear that ran through the town like a current.

Not my problem, I reminded myself. Get the girl, get the money, get a ship, find my brothers. The grounders would have to take care of themselves.

In the back of my mind, I could feel Doc's disapproving gaze.

Sure, she'd been a rogue mad scientist tampering with the very nature of life, but she was also an idealist. She wanted to build and experiment without someone looking over her shoulders, but she believed that unfettered science could create untold wealth for the masses of forgotten people in the Empire.

I'd never paid too much attention to her when she got on a political rant, but looking around as I emerged from Xavis' head-quarters onto the street, I had to agree. It was ridiculous for the Empire to worry about what she was doing, when it couldn't even keep colony planets from turning into the outright property of crime lords, bosses, and gangs.

Still. Not my problem. I already had one crusade. Someone else would have to take this one.

The furthest location on the list Xavis had provided me of possible places to find the girl was an old diner, nearly on the other side of the city.

I headed that way, letting the noise and the chaos of the city wash over me, stretching my senses to filter it all. It was all information, pattern, and flow. Even in the wreck of a city like this, normal people went around doing their normal things. It was the disturbance to the flow that could be interesting.

And then I heard it, the murmur and mutter of a small crowd gathering, not far from my destination. I put on more speed, winding my way through the packed streets.

The restaurant only earned a quick glance; it was empty, silent, window to the kitchen shuttered. The sound of the crowd came from a short distance behind the restaurant, in the warren of back alleys.

As I rounded another corner, I saw them, less than ten people, muttering to themselves, pointing at something on the ground by the wall of a building.

No. Someone. Between their legs, I could see the shape of a woman. Copper skin, dark hair.

Of course.

I edged around the group. An old man and a young boy hunched over my target. She lay crumpled on the ground, a smear of blood in her hair matching one on the wall, one leg twisted to the side at a bad angle. But her breathing was better than expected, given her injuries.

I pushed my way towards her and the crowd melted, eager to fade before more trouble started.

Her eyes fluttered open and the old man helped her sit up and lean back against the building. She blinked again, looking at her two rescuers, and then she noticed me.

Her eyes widened, the deep golden brown iris surrounded almost entirely by white. The boy noticed first, spinning around to face me.

"Leave her alone," he snarled, or would have, if it hadn't come out in a high voice, tense with fear. What he lacked in years, he seemed to make up with intensity.

A low, raspy voice called him back. "Bani, I need you."

He instantly went to her side, still glaring at me.

"Help me stand, kiddo." Between the boy and the wall, she pushed herself upright. The strain was written clearly on her face, but she didn't fall.

The old man, gray hair plaited down his back, moved between us. "Sir, whoever you're working for, surely you can see that she's injured. Give her time to recover, please."

The girl may have pissed off Xavis, but she wasn't short of defenders. They wouldn't really do her any good, but it was a nice thought.

"Artin, can you get Bani some food?" the girl asked, apropos of nothing. "I promised him a feast, and I'd hate to go back on my word."

The boy protested, whispering hotly.

She nodded and moved her hand from his shoulder to lean entirely on the wall. "But I need you to help Artin. I need someone I trust, Bani."

She grinned, and the slight twist of her lips transformed her entire face. Not a beauty, not polished like the fancy girls who roamed Xavis' complex, but a spark that shone brightly. "I can trust you, right?"

Low blow, but it worked. The boy bit his lip and looked down, scuffing his feet in the dust.

She hit him, just a light tap on the arm, but it seemed to be enough to get her point across. He tapped her back, then moved to the old man who still stood before me.

"Kara says that you need help in the shop," the boy muttered. "And that I need to eat more."

The old man glanced behind him, and the girl mouthed 'please.'

He nodded and put his arm around the boy. "And she's right. All this fuss has probably cost me customers." They moved away, and the old man took another long look at Kara, eyes sad, but accepting. "If you're good, I'll tell you about the time Kara tried to help with customers and ended up setting the shop on fire."

"Really? Cool!" the boy's voice faded away as they turned the corner.

Kara sagged against the wall. "You're from Xavis, aren't you?" No fear, just flat resignation.

"I'm to bring you to him, yes."

"Well, he's been waiting all day, I guess he can wait a little longer. It's going to take me a while."

She pushed away from the wall and took a tentative step. Her face paled, but she forced another.

"Don't be stupid," I bit out.

"It's been a stupid sort of day," she snapped back, then her leg crumbled beneath her.

For a fraction of a second, I considered letting her hit the ground, see if the pain would shock the stubbornness out of her.

It would have been the smart thing to do.

Instead, I grabbed her without thinking more, holding her tight against me. Beneath her curves were lean, strong muscles.

For the first time in far too long, my wolf strained for a different sort of chase.

KARA

J hate being weak.

But when the soldier held me to him, there was no question of his superior strength. My face buried in his broad chest, I couldn't help but get a taste of his own scent - strange, spicy, like something I'd never had before, but wouldn't mind a taste of it.

What the hell was I thinking about? I shook my head to clear it and winced at the shooting pain in my skull.

With a quick swing, he pulled me up, one arm gently supporting my knees, the other wrapped around my back.

"I'm not a child," I snapped.

He was already moving off, down through the alleys.

"Obviously."

My face flamed. While I had been getting a sense of him, how much of me had he felt?

He moved quickly through the twisted passages, deftly dodging piles of trash.

As we rounded one corner, I heard a clatter above us, but, before I could think to cry out, he bent over me, shielding me with his own back.

Unnecessarily, since he twisted away so fast that the rubbish missed us entirely. I blinked. Who moved that fast?

But bending over gave me a better look at his face, rather than just the underside of his chin.

Lightly tanned, his face had the same unlined look as many long-term space voyagers I'd seen passing through the city.

A broad jaw and sharp cheekbones brought attention to his bright green eyes. His hair was cut short, almost military. A grey knit top did nothing to hide the muscles of his chest. The soft fabric invited me to relax, and I almost rubbed my cheek against it before I caught myself.

I decided this was all the fault of the concussion.

"It'd be faster if you went down the main roads," I mumbled. I didn't want him to. Didn't want to get to Xavis' faster, didn't want people to see me carried like an infant down the streets I thought I owned.

But it would get me out of his arms faster, away from his maddening scent.

"Not likely. You have too many friends. I don't want anyone deciding to stage a rescue."

"Afraid you'll lose your prize?"

He laughed, short, brisk, more like a snort, really.

"They'd slow me down, but not much. Just don't want Xavis taking the cost of any collateral damage out of my fee."

"You're pretty damn sure of yourself." Cocky bastard.

"I have reason to be."

There wasn't much answer to that.

"You don't need to worry about a rescue. There's nowhere to run to," I whispered.

He didn't reply for a block or two.

"You should rest. We'll be there soon." His voice was softer than the words, and for the first time today, I realized there was nothing I could do, nothing I could fight. No reason to keep myself tense in his arms as if I was going to spring out at any moment. I wouldn't make it five steps. I forced myself to relax, and he gently readjusted his grip on me.

"Who are you, anyway?" The gash in my skull stabbed at me again, and I gritted my teeth. Nothing to be done about it now. "I thought I knew all of Xavis' soldiers."

"New in town. Traveling through."

Of course he was. And of course, this was how I'd met him. I'd bet he wouldn't have taken my savings, like Juda. I drifted off, half-dazed by the blow to my head, almost lulled to sleep by his steady pace.

Who had been that guy that took my haul? Another stranger, passing through? And what was with the stupid helmet? Our recyclers weren't great, but the air here was perfectly breathable.

Ghelfi City got a lot of traffic, but mostly folks looking to get rich as miners, or gamblers, hustlers. Not many folks that registered as military. Odd that today I'd run into two.

"Hey," I murmured, "Are there others like you?"

His step faltered, and the grip on me tightened. "What do you mean?"

Ugh. I really needed some sleep. "Sorry, that didn't make sense. Did other people come here with you?"

He didn't say anything, didn't really react, but I could hear his heart speed up, just a bit. A muscle twitched in his jaw before he answered. "I'm alone. There's only me."

I'd heard that a lot here. When most people said those words, they sounded bleak, empty. Lonely.

He sounded angry.

"What's your name, anyway? I'm pretty sure you know mine."

"Davien."

His hold on me relaxed again, and I drifted off into the sounds of the city around us. Delivery kids shouted at newbies to get out of the way, mini-bike horns blared. The grinding sound of repair machinery, trying to eke a few more years out of buildings that should have been discontinued. A man's voice shouted, surprised, and I heard the muffled laughter of kids up on a nearby rooftop.

"What are you smiling about?"

I rubbed my eyes. "Hadn't realized I was. Just nice, listening to the city."

"It's chaos."

"Yup. Chaos, and for once I don't have anything to do with it, or about it. Kinda nice.'"

The thought of a feast of noodles and spicy Shao sauce, pungent enough to make my tongue burn, wrapped through my mind. We must be passing by another restaurant. Nothing smelled as good as Artin's cooking, but I had to confess, there were times I'd strayed to other noodle stalls, just to try.

Puffy steamed buns, filled with chopped mushrooms. Golden fried rolls, hot enough to burn your fingers when you dipped them, tall cold glasses of...

"Ow!" I grabbed my head, the pain jolting me fully awake. "You shook me!"

"You can't go to sleep, not with a head injury." He didn't sound remorseful at all. "Don't you know better?"

"I always sleep it off when I get hurt. What are you going to do, kiss it and make it better?"

DAVIEN

$\mathcal{I}$ stumbled at her words, and she winced at being jarred. "Sorry about that." What the hell was I doing, apologizing to prey?

Just traveling through, I reminded myself. Not getting involved, even if her scent was unlike any other I'd found on Neurea. Tired, in pain, an edge of despair, but whatever fear she had wasn't of me.

She remained silent the rest of the way.

As we entered the ground floor of the complex, she struggled in my arms. "Let me down," she whispered. "I can stand on my own."

I kept my grip and entered the tube, striding past the low-level minions waiting for new orders. No one tried to join us in the car. The retinal scanner ID'd me. "Sub 7," I answered the chime.

As we descended, I lowered her to her feet. She put weight on the left leg gingerly, then pulled back sharply. "Broken?" I visually examined it through the tight brown leggings she wore. The cosh on her head could have masked the smell of other injuries, but I didn't see any other spilled blood.

She rocked back to her left leg, then the right. "Just twisted, I think." She shrugged. "But it's not really going to matter."

Something about her flat acceptance of her fate crept under my skin like an itch I couldn't scratch.

"You're not even going to fight for your life?" I taunted.

She stared at me, anger burning in her eyes. "What the hell did you think I was doing?"

The tube chimed again, signaling our arrival. She pushed past me, shoving open the doors, then stopped cold.

Xavis reclined in his hover chair, legs splayed open to accommodate the head of the scantily clad brunette kneeling before him. Hands fisted in her hair, he fucked her mouth savagely.

The sucking sounds filled the room, underscored by her muffled gags. Xavis kept his eyes fixed on her face, and I idly wondered if he was as excited by her humiliation as her work on his cock.

Either way, he finished quickly and waved us to the base of the dais while the brunette cleaned him up and shuffled away.

Xavis focused on Kara, sharp gaze missing nothing. "You're wounded. Medic!"

From a side door, a pale man emerged, carrying a small black case. He knelt to the side of Kara and began to examine her.

Once summoned, Xavis ignored him. "You can explain while he works."

I stayed silent by her side while the medic activated the scanner, then pulled out a basic regenerative cuff. Kara leaned against me, trying to keep her weight off the leg. Xavis might have assumed I remained close to execute his judgment. He could think whatever he liked.

"You've never been late before. What happened?" His voice was tinged with the slightest worry, something I'd never heard from him before.

"There was... a complication." I could feel her tense against me. Something she didn't want to reveal. Interesting. The medic moved to heal the crack on her head, and I could see her thinking, using the distraction to decide how much to reveal. "My funds weren't as solid as I thought."

"What aren't you telling me?" Xavis asked. Again, not a stupid man.

"Nothing." She bit her lip. "It doesn't matter. I had a backup plan." For a moment, her sparkle was back. "You would have loved it. Slow-timed acid mini-bombs. Been working on it for a while."

"Hmm... anything I might hear about from another source?"

She flashed a grin, then flinched as the medic manipulated her knee again. "Maybe. But there's no trace on antonium dust."

"Antonium. Really." He almost purred. "How much did you get?"

He smiled, and I began to relax. Maybe this would work out. The girl would be safe, I'd get my payment and be that much closer to getting off this rock.

"Eight vials."

Xavis brought the hover chair down to her level. "My girl, I knew I was right to put my trust in you."

The medic bowed to Xavis and scurried away, job done.

She rocked back and forth on her legs again, testing, before she answered.

"I don't have it anymore." There it was, the braced posture from the holo.

His eyes narrowed. "What do you mean, my dear?" The ice had returned to his voice.

She took a deep breath. "I had it, had it stashed safe. But when I came back to it, some weird guy had found my stash."

Xavis shook his head. "I taught you better than that. A sloppy job, no doubt."

"No!" she flared. "It was well and truly hidden. I don't know how he found it, sensors for the dust, something. And there was something odd about that guy. Wrong."

Xavis waved a hand, obviously bored. "So many things in

Ghelfi are wrong. Luckily the Waste is always available to erase these little mistakes."

"Wait!" she cried, fear slicing through her voice. "I'd know this guy again. Black uniform, totally new, no marks. And a helmet, too dark to see through, but he wore it around like he needed it to breath."

I froze, for the second time today caught off guard. Mind spinning, I only half heard the next lines.

"Fairy tales and lies are no good." Xavis snapped, and two enforcers stepped forward. "Escort my ex-protégée to the Waste. She should have learned there's no room for failure here."

They were halfway across the room before my brain snapped back into gear.

"No."

Xavis looked at me, brow cocked. "I must have misheard you in my sorrow. Please repeat yourself?"

The idea only half-formed, I plunged ahead. "You've obviously invested in the girl. Why waste all of it? Just punish her instead."

His eyes narrowed, considering. "I suppose you've thought of a suitable punishment? Something that will ensure no one else follows her example?"

I grinned, baring my teeth. "Give the girl to me."

I felt the shock run through her body. She moved, but I pulled her back in front of me, pressing into her, ignoring her fists as they rained on my shoulder.

"No one willing to play with you, Davien?" he chuckled.

I pulled her to me, thrust my mouth onto hers. She struggled against me, and I could hear Xavis' breathing getting heavy as he watched us. My tongue forced open her lips, ravishing her mouth until she gasped against me. She tasted of blood and strawberries.

I stood straight, crushing her to me. "I'll take her, use her, get your dust. I'll keep half."

Xavis licked his lips, calculating.

"You'll have made an example of her, and be ahead. Or, you can toss her into the Waste and have nothing."

She struggled. "Xavis, no. You know I'll be good for the tithe. Don't do this…"

But he wasn't listening to her anymore.

"Take her. You have three days. And then I'll send the rest of the enforcers after you both." Xavis' grinned evilly. "I don't think you've made many friends during your time here."

With a speed that surprised me, Kara pulled away, making a break for the door. I caught her, pressed her against the wall, her tight ass nestled against my cock. Rings, the scent of her was going to kill me. I grabbed her wrists and held them in one hand, over her head, while the other hand bent her head towards me.

"Don't ever run from me," I whispered. I licked the outer curve of her ear, then bit lightly, just enough to make her quiver beneath me. "You don't want me to chase you."

KARA

he shock of his words nearly brought me to my knees. He backed away from the wall, giving me just enough space to fall back against him.

He scooped me up, but this time instead of the despair I had felt as he carried me injured through the streets, waiting for Xavis' judgment, this time I was hyperaware of the feel of his hands against my body.

I'm going to blame it on the head injury again.

But, really, all I could think of was how his hands had felt against me, the fire where his body pressed into mine, how his mouth at my ear had taken my breath away, turned my core liquid.

Head whirling, I didn't think to run until he had brought us quickly through a maze of corridors. It was only when the door slid closed behind me and I realized I was in his chamber that my mind snapped back into place.

I bucked in his arms, but couldn't break free. With two quick strides, he carried me the width of the room and dropped me on the narrow bed.

"Don't touch me," I spat. Scrambling from the bed, I ducked

and rolled, trying to dodge him to get to the door. My hand slapped against the control panel, but nothing happened.

I slapped it again, still no response. The bastard had fixed it for his bio imprint.

I spun and glared at him, my hand slowly easing down my hip. "I'm not a whore."

Through it all, he stood in the middle of the room, arms crossed over his chest, one eyebrow cocked over an otherwise immobile face. "I never thought you were." He smirked. "That's what's going to make this so much fun."

"You bastard," I reached for my knife and lunged towards him, then paused. Shit. I didn't regret saving Bani, but, damn, I wished I still had my knife.

I could fight anyway. I charged him, and then ducked low with the spinning kick that swept his feet out from under him.

If I had to beat him into submission and then use his hand while he was unconscious to open the door, so be it.

I quickly scanned the room, looking for something, anything heavy to use as a bludgeon. But other than the bed and a small jump bag, there was nothing. Fine, I could work with that.

His hand snagged my ankle. I strained against him, reaching for the bag. Surely there would be something in there I could use.

There had to be, otherwise, I was out of options.

My fingers brushed the edge of the flap, then, with one smooth jerk, he pulled me away. I flipped to my back, aiming a kick at his chest with my free leg.

He caught me as I swung, and knelt above me, both ankles now trapped by his hands.

"Just calm down and listen," he said. He wasn't even breathing hard.

I pulled my knees towards me as hard as I could, twisting to snap back against his grip.

"Fine," he growled. "If that's how you want to play it."

His hands slid down my legs, pulling me closer to him.

Thumbs dug into the tight muscles of my thighs, while I fought to sit up. One massive hand planted itself to the side of my head, and then he was on top of me, face inches above mine.

"If you'd listen," he started, but I didn't want to listen. I wanted to fight, I'd been fighting all day, fighting to stay safe, and it was all I knew how to do.

Like a star bursting in my mind, it clicked.

I wasn't dead. I wasn't in the Waste.

I was alive, and alive felt good. He felt good. Smelled good, too.

The hard length of him pressed into me, and on impulse, I rocked my pelvis up to meet him.

His breath shuddered. "What are you..." A muscle tightened in his throat, disappearing down the neck of his shirt. My tongue darted out, traced the line of it. He tasted of sweat and spice.

"Don't do that." The words were soft in my ear. "Don't start something you won't want to finish."

I nipped his neck instead of answering.

In response, his mouth fell on me, sucking, biting from the ear down my throat and back, sparks of lightning burning my skin. I wrapped my arms around his broad back, arching against him. My hands tugged his shirt out from his pants, desperate to feel more of his skin.

His lips moved to mine, tongue teasing, flicking against my own. The hell with that. I pulled his head towards me, daring him to meet me, lost in the fire.

The feel, the taste of him, the air left me and I didn't care and all I wanted was more....

Until a sudden beeping filled the room.

He froze and rolled off me to kneel next to the travel bag while I lay there, panting.

"What the hell is that?" I asked, mind still reeling.

His fingers flew over the screen of a small tablet, and long minutes passed until he answered. "That," he said, putting the tablet back into the bag, calm demeanor firmly back in place, "is what I want to talk to you about."

"You've got a funny way of getting a girl's attention," I griped, pushing myself up to sit propped against the bed.

That smirk again. "I didn't notice you were objecting."

"Well, according to your little deal with Xavis, it wouldn't have mattered," I snapped back.

He held his hands out in surrender. "I need your assistance. What other deal was going to convince him not to throw you into the Waste?"

I laughed. "Doesn't look to me like you need anyone's help." I eyed him, his size, and the way people had backed away from him in the reception hall. "The rate you're going, you'll be running Ghelfi by the end of the quarter."

Revulsion cracked the ice of his face. "I don't intend to be here that long."

"Honey, no one does." I ran my hand through my hair, trying to work out the tangles, half wondering if I should just cut it shorter. "Have you seen who we make money from? Everyone thinks they're just going to be here for a while, passing through. Odds are so bad on getting out, even I don't know a bookie who'd take the bet."

"And that's what I'm talking about," he said.

I looked at him. "I've got the head injury, but you're the one not making any sense."

He sighed and relaxed back against the wall, eyes closed. For the first time, he looked like anything other than an invincible force. He looked tired.

"That thing," he stopped himself. "The man you saw in the dark helmet. Do you think you could find him again? Ask questions, see where he's staying? You know everyone in this town. They'd talk to you."

I rubbed the back of my head. Sure, the medic fixed it all up, but I wasn't looking forward to getting smacked around like that again.

He must've known what I was thinking. "I don't need you to fight it, just find it for me."

"You keep saying 'it.' You mean that thing's not human? No one's got robots that good, not even high-end androids. At least not that I've ever heard." I laughed. "But if aliens have attacked, I guess it makes sense that they'd start on the edge of the Empire."

"I don't really know, and it doesn't matter." His voice was flat. "I need to find some other people. And I think it has some information that will help. And once I have that, and enough money to buy a ship, I'm off this rock. Half of the antonium dust you took should be enough for what I need."

I let his words sink in. It was true, most everyone that came here to do a little mining, a little smuggling, or a little black market dealing thought they'd be in and out having made their fortunes. But there was a flat determination in his voice, a cold competency. I bet he could do it.

"I'll help you, but on one condition."

"Are you sure you're in a position to make demands?"

I shook my head. "That was a deal between you and Xavis. As far as I'm concerned, I can help you or not. If I don't find your guy or that dust, I'm not in any worse shape than I was before you decided to stick your head in."

His eyes narrowed. "So, what do you want?"

"I want off this planet. You don't have to take me with you wherever you're going, I just want out of here, a chance for a better life." For the second time that day, a random thread of generosity crossed through me. "Passage for both me and Bani."

He looked confused.

"The boy you saw me with earlier. You know, when you 'picked me up'?"

His eyes cleared. "What about the boy's father?"

"His father?" I tried to think back to who else had been there, what the hell he was talking about. "Old Artin? Artin's not his father. At least, I don't think so." Dammit, now I was thinking I should bargain for more people. Old Artin deserved to get out of here. Hell, so did everyone. I sat back against the side of the bed.

He looked unconvinced.

I shook my head irritably. "I can ask Bani, but, honestly, I don't think he's ever cared. Not like either of his parents have ever given him the time of day."

A look of clarity spread over his face and I realized what was up with the stupid questions.

"You thought I was Bani's mother?"

Bani was a good kid and all, but I couldn't imagine bringing a child into this world. A quick flash of memory brought my mother's pale features to me, her hand twisted, arm hanging limply off the edge of the bed.

I shoved that memory far away where it belonged.

And I sat and waited. Now that we'd cleared up that misunderstanding, the deal was up to my captor. I knew perfectly well that trying to rush things, saying anything, would only weaken my position.

His eyes flicked over to the travel bag.

"Done. You help me find it, help me get whatever information it has, as well as the antonium dust, and I will provide passage for both you and the boy off Neurea."

"Wait a minute, I don't want just any 'passage' off this planet. I don't want you to shove us into some slavers' hold."

"I will arrange passage that you find acceptable then," he grimaced. "Traveling with me may not be safe."

I snorted. "You think? Going one round with that helmeted nightmare was bad enough. If you're deliberately taking on more like that guy, I don't feel the need to be anywhere around that kind of business."

But whatever toughness I hoped had crept back into my voice was removed by the loud gurgling coming from my belly.

Smirking bastard just looked amused. "Should we continue

negotiations elsewhere?" He rose to his feet and I held my hand up for him to pull me up.

"Everyone thinks you own me now, so you're buying." The smirk disappeared into surprise. "Come on, I'll show you the best places."

DAVIEN

She moved to the door and waited, arms folded across her chest.

I reached for the biometric panel but stopped, my hand millimeters away from its surface.

"Not going to run?"

"Is there any point?"

Rings, yes. The idea of chasing her, catching her, had my blood racing, but this wasn't the time. There was never going to be a time.

"Come on," I growled. We didn't talk until we got to the elevator. An unwelcome pleasant thrill ran through me as Kara turned away from the elevator and opened the door to the stairs.

"If you don't mind, I have an errand to do on the way."

"You're the one who's hungry."

She started up the stairs. "I hate that elevator, feels like you're trapped, waiting for something bad to happen."

Behind her back, I raised an eyebrow. I thought she'd been Xavis' favorite thief, his golden child until her recent fall from grace. Why would she have such evil memories of this place?

From the moment we stepped into the stairwell, I could hear

the whispers and giggles of the children above, but we didn't see them until the third landing. I slowed, hoping that Kara would ease my presence, get us through without complications.

No such luck.

"Catch me!" A tiny figure darted out around Kara and leaped off the landing towards me.

At least this time she wasn't falling headfirst towards the sharp steps, but I didn't think it was much of an improvement as I dashed forward to catch her.

The girl nestled in my arms, and immediately resumed her inspection of my ears. "I told you they were pointy," she declared as small fingers flexed the curved tissue of the helix back and forth.

"Hoyt says that you're scary, and I should stay away, but you're not scary at all."

I took the stairs two at a time to deliver her back to her small pack. I loosened my grip on her legs but she just tightened hers around my neck. I sighed and gave up, reseating her on my forearm.

I looked around. "Where's the older boy that was with you earlier? Who's watching out for you?"

"Oh!" She unwrapped her arms around my neck to focus her attention on my lips, pushing them out of the way of her goal. "Say something again. Your teeth are pointy, too."

I caught Kara looking at us, amusement writ large over her face before her brow knotted in concern.

"That's a good question. Where is Hoyt?" She glanced our way. "Mavi, stop playing with his teeth. He really is kinda scary, lots of people think so."

Mavi wiggled to be let down and made a jump for the floor. She turned to stand in front of me, hands on hips, scowling at Kara. "He is not. He's nice. And I'll kick anyone who says any different!"

Kara blinked.

I shrugged. There didn't seem much else to do.

"Whether he's scary or not, right now I need to know where Hoyt is." She looked at the older kids, scanning across their faces. "He wouldn't have left without telling at least one of you."

One finally shoved the hair out of his eyes, her eyes, couldn't tell. "He went to get some food. He won't be gone long."

Kara frowned. "I'll come by later tonight and check on you."

As I followed her up the rest of the stairs I could hear her muttering. She was right, the situation sucked, but it didn't seem like an issue anyone was going to do anything about anytime soon.

Once we reached the slightly fresher air of outside, she headed back the way we had come that morning.

"Have you eaten at Artin's yet? Best curry and ramen house in the dome."

She threaded her way through the crowds of the main thoroughfare. I stayed a step behind her, watching. Folks nodded, waved at her, then looked at me with eyes narrowed. Word had apparently gotten around about my deal with Xavis, and the general opinion wasn't favorable.

"So," she said, tossing the words back over her shoulder as she darted around the edge of a cart selling used and modified household cleaning robots, "tell me about Helmet Head."

"What?"

"Helmet Head. Unless you've got another name for that guy?"

Her words brought an unexpected catch to my throat. Doc Lyall had called them the Swarm, they'd called themselves Hunters. But as long as they delivered the money and parts she needed, she hadn't paid that much attention to them.

Helmet Head was as good a name as any. But before I could answer, we had arrived at the front of a small storefront. A starched blue and white curtain hung down halfway covering the door, and I had to admit the smell of whatever was cooking inside promised better things than anything I'd had since I left the *Daedalus*.

"Order, then talk." Kara pushed through the curtain.

I followed, unsurprised to see the older man who had been crouching over her still form when I first found her.

Was that really just this morning?

By the glare he sent me, I could add him to my fan club as well. He bustled out from behind the counter to wrap Kara in a fierce hug.

"I'm okay, just starving." But she hugged him back.

He moved back behind the counter. "You want your regular, honey?"

"I want three of my regular. I'm really, really hungry." She tilted her head towards me. "Besides, he's paying."

Ice covered his face as he turned to me, waiting. Aha. I held out a credit chip for him to scan.

"I can't afford for people to eat and run."

"Unless it's her?" I risked a slight smile.

His face softened. "She's always good for it." He chuckled. "One way or another."

Kara sat at one of the two tiny tables wedged at the front of the shop.

Artin turned to the back of the restaurant. Instead of the grinding of a replicator starting, I heard the sizzle of oil hitting a hot pan.

Kara grinned, eyes bright. "I told you, he's the best in the dome. He may start with some replicated ingredients, but he actually knows how to cook."

The pungent scent filled the room and my own belly began to grumble. She laughed. "See, you're human after all. No matter what weird cosmetic mods you have." She sipped from the steaming cup of tea Artin had placed before her. "Honestly, it's not a bad idea, if you're planning to continue a career as an enforcer."

She wasn't the first to assume that my... peculiarities were simple cosmetic modifications.

At least mine were more practical than iridescent tattoos that slithered along my skin, or implanted horns sprouting from my skull, or any of the number of things I'd seen. All of those only changed the surface. Doc had made our changes much deeper.

Artin brought us steaming bowls, piled high with noodles. "You finish that, and I'll bring you the next." He patted Kara on the shoulder as he left.

I looked at the bowl in front of me, noodles mixed with some vegetables I didn't recognize and long slices of fungus. I poked pale cubes of something spongy with my chopstick.

"Bean curd," Kara answered my unspoken question. "Good for you."

She shoveled noodles with disturbing rapidity, not seeming to care about the scalding heat.

"I thought you wanted to come here because it was good. Can you even taste anything when you're eating that fast?"

"I'll taste the next bowl. Didn't eat yesterday, either. Was working."

And then the fruits of her job were taken by a Hunter. Not a good few days for her.

I took a tentative sip of the broth. Spicy and sour, the taste exploded on my tongue with more strength than any rations I'd had before. It wasn't long before I found myself eating almost as fast as Kara.

She glanced up. "I told you so."

Artin took the bowls and brought two others. This time she ate more slowly, savoring the deep orange curry. "I can listen now. Start talking. What do you want me to do?"

"I want you to find information about Helmet Head." I kind of liked the name, to be honest. "To begin with, is it staying in the dome, if so, where, and is it alone?"

She kept eating but her eyes were fixed on me, processing.

51

"If you find its lair and you get a chance to snag any of its tech, anything that looks like a communications pad, anything light and easy, go for it. But no stupid risks."

"I've already fought it once. I'm not eager to go another match." She took another sip of tea. "What about the antonium dust? Right now, we both need that."

"If it's an easy score, grab it. Otherwise, if you find it, let me know, and I'll take care of it."

"You're going to take it on?" Her eyebrows rose. "I know you're tough and all, but that seems stupid."

"Right now, I just need information. If anyone can find out where that thing is hiding, you can. People will talk to you."

A few more bites of curry disappeared while she thought. "Fine. But I don't want to go back to Xavis' unless we have to. Meet me here in six hours. I should have something by then."

She pulled out her commlink and bumped her codes to mine. "Don't call unless you have to."

She finished her meal in silence, then leaned back, stretching contentedly.

Artin brought over two plates this time, empty save for a small bright orange sphere, dusted with white powder. "I know you said you wanted three, but I've never known you to make it past two bowls before you're ready for your sweet."

She laughed, and he walked away to wait on another couple that had come into the shop.

I looked at the orange ball warily. She rolled her eyes.

"Seriously? You think you're going to take on Helmet Head and you're afraid of dessert?"

She picked hers up and I could see that sphere was slightly soft, her fingers sinking into it slightly.

"Like this." She took a bite, revealing the pale peach jelly filling within. Her eyes closed. "Mmmmn," she sighed.

I stared at her face an instant too long and then returned my attention to the far safer dessert in front of me. I cut off a small piece to sample. Good, but too sweet.

I placed the sphere back on the plate and offered it to her. "Not quite to my liking, I'm afraid."

That, and if I was going to deal with one of the Hunters, I'd at least enjoy watching her eating one more dessert first.

Before she finished, I could hear a faint whisper from the woman standing at the other corner of the shop, waiting for her order. "You heard what happened, right?"

The man responded. "It's not really a huge surprise, is it? You know what they say about her mother."

My eyes swept the room. There was no one else here, and although their backs were to us, it seemed their comments were pointed. Old Artin hadn't heard anything over the sizzle of the cooking, but from the pale look on Kara's face, I could tell the comment had struck home.

"Let's get started. I can't do anything in here." With a quick wave at Artin, she pushed out through the curtain without waiting for me.

I caught up with her outside. "What was that about?" I asked.

She spun and struck me in the chest. "You buy me. To use as a whore. In public. And you don't think people are going to be talking about it?"

I cocked my head. "I did explain that was the only way to get you out of there, right? You know the truth. I know the truth. Why do you care?"

She dug her fingers through her short hair, pulling at it in frustration. "It won't matter. I'll do the job, you'll get the dust, and I'll be the hell off this rock."

Just as fast, she spun away again, slipping through the crowd.

I stared at her for a long minute after she disappeared. What a stupid thing to waste energy on.

But I had other things on my schedule today.

The alert on my tablet back at Xavis' complex had served as a reminder of that.

I made my way through back alleys, folded in on myself a little, stooped, not walking quite as fast.

It was one thing for people to remember Davien, the enforcer when he was out on a job. At the moment, I'd rather fade from memory. Finally, the gray tinted edge of the dome with a large airlock into the Waste came into sight.

Another 'lock served the landing pad that brought newcomers into the dome, but it was far too busy for my purposes. The lack of traffic here meant I just needed to do a little waiting.

I crouched behind a pile of trash and settled for a long rotation. There's more of a trick to staying still, staying patient, than people believe.

You must put your mind on hold, keep it distracted from any urge to move, to fidget. Keep it disassociated from any of the petty demands of the body. But still remain alert and aware of who is passing by, of the weather, of sounds. And, most importantly, aware of your target.

A low rumble announced what I'd been waiting for. Without moving, I flexed each of my cramped muscles in succession, slowly bringing the blood pumping back and recalling my limbs to life. I couldn't risk a stumble.

The large trucks that daily passed through the 'lock could be filled with passengers for another city or miners out to their job or, really, any of a number of things.

It didn't really matter to me.

What did matter was they had a nice high clearance.

As the nose of the truck passed my hiding place, I edged around the pile of trash. In the instant the windowless back half of the truck drew parallel to me, I rolled between the last pair of wheels and reached up with hands and feet to pull myself into the undercarriage.

The truck rumbled through the first gate of the airlock. It

closed behind us and for the moments it took for the chamber's breathable air to be pumped back into the dome, I remembered Kara's terror of being thrown into the Waste.

With good reason. Humans couldn't survive the toxic atmosphere out there, not for more than a few moments.

The exterior doors slid open, and my ride rumbled out into the night.

KARA

$\mathcal{I}$ pushed through the crowd, shame scorching my cheeks. How dare he not understand? My jaw ached from biting back the scream that I'd longed to fling at him. And that stupid, know-it-all smirk.

Except.

I wasn't in the Waste, and other than his annoyingly cocky manner, Davien, the terrible enforcer, really didn't seem to be that bad of a guy.

I giggled, causing a passing miner to look at me oddly.

Just remembering little Mavi's fierce defense of her protector was enough to add a slightly surrealist twist to a day that had already gone completely off the rails.

Besides, whatever people thought of me, it wouldn't matter for long. I had a plan.

Locate Helmet Head, get the information, get the dust, get away, and start a new life.

Step one: Find Helmet Head. I looked around. I hadn't really thought through my direction when I stormed away, more concerned with getting away from that smirk.

Who did I know around here that might have information? I

looked up at the storefront across the way from me. I'd seen the owner from time to time, but she kept her head down and stayed out of trouble. But...

Across the front of the store were three clusters of micro cams.

Maybe I didn't need to find people who had seen Helmet Head. Maybe I just needed to talk to the one person who saw everything.

I headed back to the main street and then grabbed the tram line as it passed, heading towards the spaceport.

I jumped off well before the edge of the dome and worked my way in a zigzag pattern through the blocks. The buildings around here had been erected by some gambler years ago in hopes of a thriving space commerce plan panning out. But, like most things, it had fallen through and now the buildings were either crumbling or gang hangouts or divided into multifamily units.

Or at least, most of them were.

My destination was a rough looking building with blacked-over windows, no different than any other on the block.

I pushed a fragment of permasteel to the side and pressed my hand to the hidden bio plate, and waited.

If I didn't know Rati never went out, I might've given up. But she didn't, so there was nothing to do but be patient. Even if she was in the middle of a project, she'd get the alert eventually. She couldn't afford to not be aware that someone was at the door. I'd have to trust she'd check the cams before starting a security sequence.

I had just settled down with my back into the alcove when a recessed light glowed green above me. I scrambled to my feet before the door slid open, spilling me into the hall.

Inside, dust and crates were all that greeted me. I very carefully followed the faint green light as it moved above me, flickering from one diode to the next, guiding me down a path between the debris in echoing silence.

I was pretty sure I had come through the maze of boxes a

different way last time, but she'd probably already booby-trapped that entry.

Another door, another bio print, another wait.

Finally, the wall slid open and I stepped on to the maglev plate that dropped me below to Rati's laboratory.

Bots of all sizes slid and scurried across the floor as I went, some cleaning, some carrying parts to various projects Rati had devised throughout her complex, mostly occupied in incomprehensible tasks.

"You're looking better than I had expected, giving how your day seems to have been going," a small box on the table next to me commented.

I kept going. "The day's been full of surprises. Can't wait to tell you all about it."

Low tables lined the path, filled with a mind-boggling array of parts - some stacked high for the bots to sort, some arranged neatly. Most were in the assorted-jumble stage.

"I'm almost done resetting this, come on back."

I walked through a light antiseptic vapor, pausing to make sure the mist covered me completely.

Sure, Rati was paranoid. But she had better reasons to be than a lot of other folks.

And she was brilliant enough to make sure she stayed safe.

I could barely make her out beneath the gleaming metal device pulled over her head and shoulders. Her hands and forearms were encased in steel tubes resting in her lap. I couldn't see any movement, but from her ongoing muttered stream of "come on, come on, just a little further," I knew she was doing something.

If I was lucky, she wouldn't try to explain it to me.

Rati was brilliant. I don't mean regular everyday kind of smart. I mean a terrifying, not really sure if she was the same sort of human as I was, brilliant.

We'd met when we were kids. She'd build toys and bots to trade the other kids for food, then moved on to building bots to assist her with larger, shall we say, more interesting projects. Eventually, her bots had made enough bots that she'd been able to move away, hide away in safety and seclusion.

"There, last fiber in place. And another step accomplished."

"Are you going to tell me about it?" I asked, warily

She slid her hands out from the metal tubes and pushed the head and shoulder enclosure off.

I knew from previous experience an offer of assistance wouldn't be welcome. But my help wasn't needed. The helmet-like contraption swung away smoothly, suspended from a hook I hadn't noticed earlier.

"Do you really want me to?" She grinned, so I knew she wasn't taking my lack of interest in her what's-it to heart. "Besides, Talon and I have gone over the parameters comprehensively. If anything, he's more thorough than I am, even if it's not his project."

"Wait a minute." I froze, shocked. "Who's Talon? I thought I knew everyone you did! At least, everyone who mattered."

She laughed and spun her chair, moving deeper into the warren of machinery. "Of course you do. At least, everyone who matters in Ghelfi." She rolled into the hallway and I could smell tea brewing. "I met him on the deep net waves for quasar computing. He had some interesting thoughts and I wanted to follow-up, see if I could start realizing his theory."

And that was one of the many reasons I was here.

Xavis kept a lock on most transmissions in and out of the city, just another way to control the population. Rati wasn't having any of that. By the time we were twelve, she'd figured out how to break his interference, at least on a small scale. Which brought her another source of security and income. People who wanted messages sent out without bringing them to Xavis' attention had learned she could be trusted.

Xavis' organization had made a mistake when they decided the sick little girl with the twisted body wasn't worth bringing into the Tithe. And I would be forever grateful to their short-sightedness.

The hallway opened up into a warmly lit living space. I sank into a low, padded chair, took off my boots, and tucked my feet up under me. Finally, her words clicked. "If you've been so busy with your whatever, how do you know what happened?"

She poured tea into thick cups for us, sent one over to me by a service bot. "I have a flag for recordings of any of my friends in a fight."

"Wait, you see me on the cameras all the time?"

Rati looked annoyed. "You know anyone can be tracking you all the time, right?" She flicked a finger at my comm. "That'd be the easiest way, but you don't think about it. And it's not like it's hard to get plenty of comparatives to train the engines for what a fight looks like."

I settled back down, sipped my tea. It was stupid. I'd come here because she had access to the recordings. Of course she could always see me. There never was any privacy to lose.

"So," she spun in her chair to a bank of panels in the wall behind her. "What the hell was that thing, and who took you away?" It was one of her frustrations that she'd never been able to breach the systems of Xavis' complex.

"That's what I need help with."

My voice faded. Who was Davien, anyway? What did I really know about him? I shook my head. It didn't matter. "The guy is one of Xavis' enforcers, but he's got a side job. He's cutting me in. If things go right, I'll be able to get out of Ghelfi, off Neurea."

"That's wonderful!" Her face fell, but only for a minute. "I'll miss you, but I'll make sure to set you up with a proper comm system before you leave. Heck, if you end up on a semi-civilized world, instead of this rock, it might be even easier to talk with you."

She spun back to her panel of screens. "What are you looking for? You know my cams can find it."

"The guy that attacked me. He took my bag, and I want it back. If I can, see where he's staying, and if he's got any friends."

"Should be a simple backtrack - let me get it started." Her fingers flew over the panels. As I watched her work, the knot in my belly grew, over leaving her, Artin, everyone I knew. I'd wanted this for so long, how could I be having second thoughts?

"Rati?"

"Hmmm?"

"You've made plenty of credits, right?"

"When I'm not doing freebies for friends, sure." She flashed a grin, then went back to work.

"Why haven't you ever left?"

Her hands stilled. "Where would I go?"

"Anywhere!" I sprang to my feet. "Anywhere would have to be better than here for you! You should be able to see more people without worrying about their connections! People across the empire should know how brilliant you are!" My voice fell to a whisper. "You shouldn't have to hide down here."

She stopped and rolled over to my chair to take my hand. "I'm not hiding. Maybe I was at first, but not anymore. I talk with people all over the dark web, we trade papers and notes and even have virtual joint projects. I've built a world of my own here, exactly to my specifications."

She looked around and laughed. "Not sure how I'd leave without taking it all with me." Her eyes lost focus for a moment. "Maybe if I build a ship around the lab, then tunneled below to have room for the firing thrusters...." She was actually planning it out, running through variables. "No, not viable at present."

She squeezed my hand. "I'll miss your visits, but I'm not unhappy here."

I swallowed against the lump in my throat. "Then I'll have to introduce you to more people who can visit you."

"Sure." She grinned wickedly. "If you think they can pass my security checks, go for it."

A trill broke the silence between us. "Let's see what we've got."

I winced just seeing my image smack against the wall. "Not looking forward to meeting that clown again," I muttered.

"I don't blame you." She hit a button, and the fight spooled back in reverse. A change in point of view signaled the switch to another camera, where we watched him moving down the alley, black globed head swaying from side to side.

She paused it. "Look at how his head moves, like he's got a sensor rig running for antonium," Rati murmured.

The cameras kept switching us back through the city as we watched him push through crowds, crossing the streets. A tram passed in front and the path varied only by a step.

A second trill sounded. "That's odd." The screen split to show two identically uniformed and helmeted forms. Rati leaned forward, frowning. "It's the same timestamp, but he's in two separate places."

"More likely it's just two people in the same stupid uniform," I reminded her gently. "Probably easier than teleportation."

She blinked. "Yes, quite. But still, it would have been an interesting effect..."

I shook my head, and we continued to watch. The split screen tracked both of them on the cameras, and with a few quick clicks of the keyboard, another showed their paths in contrasting colors against a simplified grid of the city.

"Look," I breathed. "That's got to be some sort of a search pattern." The screen showing the colored lines had been almost entirely filled. Between the two of them, they'd covered almost the entire grid of the dome.

A final ding signaled the end of the recording. The split screen merged into one as both Helmets stepped out of a nondescript doorway, marching away from each other without a glance behind.

"That's where I need to go." I stared at the map, memorizing the coordinates.

Rati tapped her chin with a finger. "Did you notice they never stopped? Not to eat, not to talk to anyone, they never slowed their pace. Like they're soldiers, not even human."

I shrugged, remembering Davien's comments. "Maybe they're not, maybe they're androids."

Her eyes lit up. "Get me one," she breathed, almost quivering out of her chair in her excitement. "Kara, you have to get one for me to experiment on. If they're androids, that means their owner has two. So he could spare one, right?"

I shook my head. "There is no way I'm bringing you one of those things. It nearly killed me when I just wanted my bag back. I don't think it's going to stop by for tea."

"Fine," she scowled. "I helped you."

I dropped a sisterly kiss on the top of her head. "Look, if I can bring you anything that I'm sure is safe, I will."

"Promise?"

"Promise."

I nearly skipped out into the streets.

I had an address, I knew there was more than one, I was halfway to my goal without even breaking a sweat.

Not even Artin's cooking tasted as good as this moment.

Which was why I didn't see Sary's goons before they nabbed me.

As I rounded the corner, arms wrapped around my chest like vines, pinning my own arms to my sides. I kicked back, but before I could connect with anything, the dark haired one Bani had bitten stepped in front of me.

"You've got a lot of explaining to do, bitch." And with that cheerful proclamation, he hit me and that was the last thing I remembered.

I came to sprawled in a chair, my wrists and ankles tied to the frame.

I kept my eyes closed as I scanned over my body. My temple

throbbed where the goon had hit me, but I didn't seem to be injured anywhere else. So far.

"You may as well open your eyes, thief. The monitors show you awake, and I believe them faster than I believe you."

Sary. Shit. Even though I'd known there would need to be a reckoning for the failed boost that morning, I'd really been hoping it wouldn't be today. It'd been a long, long day.

I opened my eyes, wincing against the brightness of the room.

Sary stood, leaning against the front of his desk. He was a big guy, rumor had it that he'd been a dust miner before coming back to the city to look for easier work. His muscles didn't look as if they'd softened much from his days in the Waste.

The dark-haired goon sat on the couch to the side of the office, thumbing through some magazine on a pad. From my angle, I couldn't see what it was, but, from his rapt attention, I was assuming it was either weapons or girls. Or maybe I was just stereotyping. Maybe it was all about new trends in aquaculture.

The blonde one stood in the far corner, scowling at me. I guess we hadn't made friends yet.

"Before we get down to business, I just want to let you know that was a fine job you pulled earlier today. I went back to look myself. How long had you been weakening that wall?"

"Two years," I sighed.

His eyebrows rose. "A good job, patient. I don't have to guess why you had to rush it. Nobody wanted to be late with the tithe today." No kidding. Not that it had done me any good.

Sary continued, "And I have to thank you for bringing my attention to the security weaknesses in my operation."

The banging in my head was louder than my words. I didn't get what he was saying, but he seemed to be in a reasonable mood. I wasn't in a position to argue with that.

"Charro's little habits could've ended up costing me a lot more."

Oh. Okay, that made sense.

"I don't tolerate weakness well, but I do have a soft spot for ambition." His eyes narrowed. "Tell you what. You give me back my dust, and maybe you should think about working for me. I can always use somebody who shows your level of initiative."

He laced his fingers together and stretched. "As long as they're loyal."

"As much as I would like to help you," I coughed, my throat dry.

Sary gestured to the dark-haired minion, who grumblingly put down his magazine and brought me a glass of water.

"You have to untie my hand."

"Oh no, my dear," Sary laughed. "Tev, be gentle."

With a delicacy I would not have expected, the goon brought the cup to my lips and tilted it, just enough for me to drink without choking me. The glare in his eyes let me know he'd rather be doing this differently.

I sipped slowly, thoughts racing. But when he pulled away the cup, the answer stayed the same. "Can't help you, I'm afraid. Don't have the dust anymore."

"Don't be stupid, and don't think I am." Sary loomed over me. "You don't plan something for two years and lose the goods the same day. Xavis might believe you, but you'll have to try harder."

I shook my head, but he'd convinced himself. Hell, I'd be hard to talk out of eight vials of antonium, if I thought I could get them back by threatening.

His meaty hand skimmed down the side of my body and I flinched. He stepped away, my commlink in his hand and a disgusting leer on his face. "I think she needs time to think about it, boys." The grin got wider. "Throw her in the cooler."

DAVIEN

I lowered my rate of breathing, felt my body adapt to the altered chemistry of the air. In some ways riding out this way made it easier. Other than keeping my grip tight on the undercarriage, I could relax and adjust to the thin atmosphere.

The carrier started to make a long curve around a sharp outcropping of rock. That was my signal. I released my hands and feet and fell the short distance to the rough road. The carrier rumbled over me as I rolled in the opposite direction, off running into the night.

I tried to keep my mind empty as I loped across the barren landscape, no longer worried what anyone saw. But thoughts of the blinker that had reported my pod's data run was complete spurred me on.

And, if I was honest, Kara didn't help my concentration. I gritted my teeth. I'd known her for less than a day. Why should the look of her face struck with fear or fury bother me so? Or the way that she felt in my arms, the smell and the taste of her?

I re-calculated my rendezvous time with her. I should be able to get to the pod, check the results, and get back to Artin's in plenty of time.

But I sped up a little, just in case.

An hour of running across the Waste led me to the shallow canyon where I had hidden the escape pod. I looked at the crumpled shell and winced. Not my best landing.

I lifted away the rock and debris I'd used to cover the hatch and slid into the pod. It felt like coming home. It was part of the *Daedalus*, part of my entire life up until a few short months ago.

The insistent flash of the instrument panel brought my mind back to the task at hand and I set to work.

When it was clear the *Daedalus* was going to be breached, Doc had told us to scatter at random. But that didn't mean I couldn't start filtering possibilities for survivors. I assumed my brothers had performed the same procedure I had, let the pod AI make the first jump while I punched in variables for the next, and so on until my scorched engines could go no further.

I knew how many jumps I'd been able to make. That, plus the position of the ship when we were attacked gave me a radius of the search sphere.

While Artificial Intelligence wasn't the Doc's field of expertise, the ship's systems were among the best money could buy. The pod systems were only a fraction of that, but it had been enough for me to start a series of scans. Given all of the variables possible, all of the distances we could have covered, what was left should be a list of potentially habitable rocks my brothers could've crashed on.

I called up the results and bit back a sigh as the data flowed past me. I had known the list would be long, but this would be almost impossible to physically search through.

But sulking about it wasn't going to help any. I sat up, squared my shoulders, and got to work sorting data.

Finally, I cracked my neck, back stiff from being hunched over the panels for so long. I hit the button to start another run, select more possible planets and prioritize the previous results.

If this job with Kara went well, I'd be able to get started on the search right away. And it had only taken...

Shit.

I'd gotten too absorbed in the task. I was already late. I sealed the pod, covered it hastily, cursing all the while.

Even at top speed back through the waste and rolling through the airlock with less than my accustomed caution, I was almost two hours past our agreed-upon meeting time when I made it to Artin's.

But, of course, she wasn't there.

The grate was pulled down over the doorway but I could see Artin inside, finishing straightening up for the day.

I rapped on the grate sharply.

He turned towards me and narrowed his eyes. "What do you want?"

Fantastic. I didn't expect for us to be buddies, but the suspicion could be dialed down a bit.

"I know I'm late meeting her, but did Kara say where she was going when she left?"

He shook his head. "I haven't seen her since the two of you left." Worry reached fingers of ice through my belly.

"She was supposed to meet me here," I said slowly, mind racing. "About two hours ago, but I missed the time."

He leaned back on the broom. "It hasn't been that busy. I would've seen if she'd been here."

"Can you think of any other places that I could start looking for her?" I tried to keep the worry from my voice, but he didn't need to hear it. His own concern was clearly written on his face.

He stepped closer to me. "She's not back at Xavis', is she?" Movement down the street caught his eye, and he broke into a relieved grin, looking over my shoulder. "Or ask the boy, I'd lay money she sent him with a message for you." He grinned. "No doubt, a reminder not to be late next time."

I turned as Bani continued down the block towards me. His

face was tight, eyes focused. It didn't look like he'd been sent with a lighthearted message.

He ran up to the grate, and Artin rolled it open, pulling him inside. I stepped inside behind them before Artin could close me out again.

The boy bent double, gasping for air. "They took her. Where have you been? I've looked for you everywhere."

Knives of burning steel replaced the ice. 'They' meant there was a target. 'They' meant there was someone to fight.

Artin pulled a chair from the top of the table and led the boy to it. He kept a hand on the boy's shoulder while Bani's breathing approached something closer to normal.

"What did you see?" The edge in my voice wasn't meant for the boy or the old man but they both looked at me with startled eyes.

I forced a calm veneer over my face. "It's going to be all right. I'll get her back."

The boy swallowed and nodded. I guess, if nothing else, he trusted me that far.

"Close your eyes." I tried to keep my voice gentle, even. "Go back to when you saw Kara get in trouble. Tell me everything you see, don't worry about whether or not you think it's important."

Reluctantly, the boy's eyes closed. Artin stood behind him, hand on shoulder still, anchoring him to the here and now.

"I knew there wasn't any point in looking for her after you took her", he started. "You were going to Xavis' hall, and I didn't want to know if..."

He trailed off, expression wretched. Of course, he'd assumed that she would be ejected. She certainly had expected that outcome.

"But it turned out she was fine, right?" I wanted to get him back on track.

He nodded abruptly. "When I heard she was free, looking for something, I wanted to find her, see what I could do to help. She might know lots of people, but nobody pays attention to me. I hear all sorts of things."

Artin chuckled and squeezed his shoulder. "We know you do," he interjected wryly.

"I couldn't find her in any of the usual spots, and then I thought maybe she went to see that friend of hers in the south quarter. I don't know who it is, but sometimes she heads that way and disappears from time to time."

His voice grew tight with tension. "I finally saw her coming out of a building. She looked excited, as if she'd found something, or gotten good news. She wasn't watching around her." His words were no more than a whisper. "It's all my fault."

"I somehow doubt that." I bit back a snarl, angry with myself. If she were in danger, that was my fault, no one else's.

Impatience to hear the rest of the story nipped at me, but if this kid was important enough to her that she made him part of our deal, I should probably not shake the information out of him.

"But it was. It was the guys that chased us this morning after I messed up her snatch from Sary's." His shoulders hunched into a protective curl. "One grabbed her, and the other guy clocked her hard. She went down and stayed down."

A growl escaped my clenched teeth. "Keep going," I forced out, my voice thick with rage.

"They stuffed her into an old flitter and headed west. It was a stupid thing to do, the roads are always clogged enough it's no problem following."

"How far did you follow them?" Artin asked.

Bani shook his head. "I saw them take her into the building, but I couldn't get any closer. I thought I should find someone to help." His eyes flew open, accusing. "But you weren't anywhere I could find and I didn't know who else could get her out."

I knelt in front of the chair. "You did the right thing. If I pull up a map, can you show me the building?"

He sprang to his feet. "I'll show you, come on!"

"Not a chance," I shook my head. "I can't keep track of where you are." And I don't know what I'm going to find, I thought, but didn't say the words.

His jaw clenched, but Artin stepped in. "You did your job. Let our new friend do his."

Moments later I had the address. As I ran through the half-darkened streets, I sorted through plans. Possible trap? Maybe, no way of telling.

Weapons, none. Intel, none. I grinned. Sometimes not having any options left just kept things simple.

A quarter hour later, I stood across the street, watching the building. A narrow, decorated residence, wedged between ware-houses. The buildings on either side squatted dark and silent, but a light shone from the second story window of the red and black facade in the middle.

Good to know where to start.

A soft scrape behind me caught my attention, and I whirled into a fighting stance.

"How the hell did you get here so fast?"

Bani shrugged. "Shortcuts."

Damn it. I couldn't leave him here; unattended he was just waiting to turn into a hostage. But if he came with me, I'd need to tone things down a bit.

"Fine," I snapped. "Follow close, don't get in the way, and don't be stupid."

He nodded, tight face a grim reminder of what he'd already seen in the city, in Xavis' hall.

The biopanel at the side of the door would take seconds to bypass. If I had my tools. As it was...

"Stay close," I grunted, then sprinted across the street, up the steps and threw my shoulder against the door. With a scream of twisted metal, it crumpled and sagged in the frame.

I stepped through into a sparsely furnished entryway. A small side table sat to the left of the door. Another hall continued ahead, and to the right were the stairs to the second floor.

I stretched my senses to their limits, but all I heard was yells punctuated by the sound of chairs being pushed hastily aside above us. Upstairs it was.

Bani followed, eyes wide, but mouth shut.

I kept to the outer wall, taking the steps in twos and threes until we reached the landing seconds after busting through the outer door. Through a door to the first room of the upper level stepped an enforcer type - short, light-colored hair, thick neck, not a lot of shine in the eyes.

Apparently, the boss here hired for brawn, not brains. Good.

His lips curled as he dismissed me to call out over his shoulder. "It's just one guy, whaddya..."

Whatever he was going to ask the person in the room was lost as I grabbed his wrist and spun him away. Locking his arm behind his back I shoved him into the wall, hard enough that flakes of spray-seal fell to the ground around him.

My other hand wrapped around the back of his throat, forcing him to face downstairs.

"This one of them?" I asked Bani, crouched a few safe steps away.

He nodded, face pale. "He's the one that hit her," he whispered.

Red flooded my vision and I squeezed, crushing the back of his skull under my fingers. With my other hand, I pulled his arm further behind his back until, with a wet wrenching noise, it popped from the socket. The screaming dwindled into a low moaning and then stopped.

"Two of them," I muttered, then threw the man's body through the open door.

I burst through the door behind him, rolling to the left out of instinct born of the slightest of noises. A chair lay on its back on the other side of the room, and near the back wall, a desk shielded a gray-haired man, caught half-standing.

A spray of pellets hit my goon, followed by cursing from both my opponents.

I swept my leg behind the blond's blaster-toting friend, then came up to a low fighting stance. This one at least had the skills to twist as he fell, avoiding landing on his ass entirely. But a jump and a pair of quick front kicks sent his weapon flying and snapped his head back hard.

I grabbed his weapon and rolled again, this time towards the chair at the other side of the room. My initial glimpse hadn't shown any opponents other than the third man, or any other exits, but a little more intel wouldn't hurt.

Besides... I looked at the slumped form of my first target, then his friend stretched out on the floor. Neither of them was going to be answering questions anytime soon.

I stood slowly, eyes locked on the older man. I'd been in town long enough to recognize Sary, Xavis' top boss, or top rival, depending on who you listened to.

He cradled a full-sized phasor before him, one hand confidently curled around the trigger. "Watch where you're going, boy."

I stepped towards him. "Not really seeing anything in my way."

Sary laughed at that. "You're Xavis' new guy, aren't you?" He looked me up and down appraisingly. "Why don't you come work for me?"

"Don't we both work for Xavis?" I asked, and took another step.

His grip tightened on the blaster. "Don't be stupid. You know that's just a formality. I run my businesses my way. The tithe is just a formality." He shrugged, eyes cold. "And who knows, Xavis may not always be the one collecting."

I shook my head and took another step. "So, taking the woman was all your idea? Part of your business?"

Sary's hand flexed, just a micrometer, but enough for me to react before he could complete the movement. The pellets of my phasor knocked the weapon from his hand, his short burst of fire striking the wall to my side.

I vaulted over the desk to smash his face against its heavy top. "I'd go easy on you, but, as you said, you run your own business. So, taking Kara comes back to you." I leaned a bit more, fighting to keep the rage down. "Where is she?"

"Filthy bitch stole from me," he grunted. "Fuck you."

I reached down and broke the pinky of his left hand. "Try again."

He hissed in pain. "You're a dead man." His low voice was still far too controlled.

"I don't think you're listening to me." I broke two more digits in quick succession and waited.

"You can't do this," he screamed, spittle flecking his lips.

I crunched the next finger, feeling it snap. "All day long, actually. Where is she?"

He glared at me from the corner of his eye but said nothing.

I leaned over to whisper in his ear. "You have two choices. Tell me where she is, and live. Or play this stupid game, and I'll carve you into pieces so small the Empire's best regenerator wouldn't know where to start."

Sary stared at the wall, silent.

"Time to start with larger joints, then." I moved my grip to his elbow, and finally, he flinched.

"I'll kill you for this," he gasped.

"You're welcome to try," I acknowledged. "But after I get the woman out."

In the end, it didn't take much to win his 'cooperation.' One thing we'd learned doing errands for the Doc was that most big men have very little trouble ordering others to take punishments but seldom can stand up to receive it.

I wrenched Sary to his feet, and with a little more encouragement, he showed us a secret panel in the wall that silently slid open before us.

"A hidden lift tube," Bani breathed.

Damn. I'd forgotten he was there.

Not that he was some innocent, but a part of me regretted he'd seen me do all of that. Not that my brothers and I had experienced some idyllic childhood, but I always thought kids should be left out of the work, if possible.

I glanced down to check on him, only to find see him glaring at Sary, eyes blazing with hate.

Well then. Maybe I was worried over nothing.

As we stepped inside the cramped space, Sary shielded the keypad with his body and entered a code. Amateur. Not even nine digits long, and he'd left the sound option active on the keypad.

I kept the older man's body in front of us as we stepped off, just in case of unpleasant surprises. But only the near-silent hum of machinery greeted us on the empty floor.

"What is this place?" Bani asked.

"My secret, little rat. You and your enforcer friend picked the wrong side." Sary laughed, the sound oily and grating.

A yelp broke off the noise as Bani kicked him in the knee.

"Dammit, kid, he's already a pain to carry."

Sary pointed to one of a line of doorways. "She's in there."

After the keypad and hidden lift tube, I was surprised that a simple biolock was the only security by each of the doors. I guess he thought if you got this far, you were supposed to be here. Definitely an amateur.

He slapped his palm against the plate and a blast of foggy cold air rolled out as the door slid open.

"She's inside," his voice whining now. "Take the bitch and go."

My mind blanked. I threw Sary against the wall, no longer caring what the kid saw or didn't.

If the old bastard had left Kara in here, if she'd been in the freezing cold for the hours since Bani saw her taken...

"Stay here," I grunted. "Watch that the door doesn't close behind me."

The shock on Bani's face let me know he'd realized the grim possibilities.

Inside, I searched through the freezing fog. A small room, easily missed in a search, if there had been a police force or any sort of authority to look. Crates and boxes all about as wide as my forearm lined one wall and part of the other.

Nothing. Across the back of the wall, a shelf held more of the boxes. I turned, ready to wake Sary by any means necessary, make him show us where she really was, when I saw it.

Just the toe of a leather boot sticking out from under the shelf, behind a row of boxes.

I swore at myself, knocking the boxes to the side, spilling small bags of some greyish powder in my haste to reach her.

"What?" Bani yelled from the doorway.

"Stay back." Kara looked so small, curled under the shelf, stripped of all her life and energy. Mottled purple surrounded one eye, giving her face the only color.

I laid my hand gently on her neck. Damn, she was like ice. And although I waited for a pulse, nothing. I bowed my head, still crouched over her. Sary, Xavis, they would all pay. It would be a delay, but she was worth it. She'd died, getting information for me. Avenging her would be my honor.

I blinked. The faintest of movements.

There it was again.

A heartbeat, weakened and thready, but there. With no more time for thought, I stripped off my jacket and wrapped it around her, then lifted her in my arms.

"Come on, kid," I said softly. "Let's get her home."

One more fucking hassle. The tube had slid closed behind us, the shock of finding Kara in the cold had distracted me. And instead of the keypad I'd so helpfully memorized the code for, another biolock mocked me next to the opening of the tube.

Bani looked between me, the lock, and the unconscious form of Sary.

"I can't carry her," his voice was harder than it had been ten minutes ago. "But I can do this." He roughly dragged Sary's unconscious body to the lift tube and wrenched the torso up until the man's palm was flat against the plate.

A soft chime congratulated him.

Bani dropped Sary back to the hard floor without a second glance.

We stepped into the lift tube and left the house, silent and grim.

"Lead on, kid," I asked him, forcing my eyes away from her too-still face, willing her to wake, to move even the slightest bit.

"What?" he stopped on the pavement, face blank.

"I don't know where she lives. We need to get her home."

"You mean, she's not..." His voice cracked, and I swore at myself again.

"No, she's not dead." Yet, the evil voice in the back of my head chimed in. "But we need to get her warm and safe, as soon as possible."

He slumped against the wall, his breath in long gasps. "I thought I was too late, that I should have gone in without finding you, that because of me she'd died."

"Knock it off," I growled. "You did good. Now, keep it up, okay?"

He nodded and headed through the side streets.

I mapped our path with only half my mind, watching her for any growing signs of life, to no avail. For the second time in one long day, I carried her through the streets of Ghelfi. I wanted her angry, even hating me, rather than so cold and still.

We turned into a dark building I would have thought long abandoned but for the faint rustling in the farthest rooms of the ground floor.

Then up a flight of stairs so cramped I had to pull her in closer so her legs didn't hit the walls.

"Sorry," Bani muttered. "The lift tube has never worked, long as I remember."

At the top floor, the air was stuffy. Only one closed door faced us, the rest opening onto storage rooms.

"Can you take her hand," I asked him, eyeing the grimy lock plate.

Bani laughed. "No need." He lifted a small, thin piece of metal from where it had lain hidden under debris at the bottom of the wall facing the stairs, and slid it between the edge of the door and the frame. A series of twitches, and then a click. He pulled the metal shim out as the door jerked open, the mechanism groaning.

I shook my head, but he just shrugged. "The lock's never worked, either. She always said she didn't want to waste money on it."

Jaw clamped firmly shut, I stepped through, eyes sweeping the room for any other threats.

But what greeted us, I'd never have anticipated.

Deepest black covered the walls and ceiling, studded with tiny lights. The positions were all wrong, but if I didn't know the charts, it would have been easy to imagine I walked under a night sky.

A click, and a soft pink column glowed. Bani stood next to a narrow bed. I glanced around.

Other than the bed, the room was almost empty. The only furnishings were painted in the same deep black, fading into the wall. But I could make out a small dresser and, next to it, a table. From the stylus and tablet placed carefully in the middle, I assumed that she used it as a standing desk. The cleansing booth and other necessaries were in the far corner, partially blocked by a half-wall.

And that was all.

I lowered her gently onto the mattress and eased off her boots. Her feet were blue-gray and when I held them gently between my palms to try to get some warmth back into her, their coldness sent ice through my hands.

"Where're her things?"

Bani moved next to me to watch as I alternated between her feet, hoping for any reaction.

"She's never had any. It's always been this way."

I glanced around again. No family mementos, no trinkets. Nothing that made the space her own, other than the painting of the night sky.

How long had she scrimped and saved to get off this planet?

Her feet began to show the first tinges of blush, signs blood flow was returning.

I tucked them under the covers and carefully laid my jacket on top, adding its weight to the thin blankets.

Her hands didn't look quite as bad. Maybe she'd had the presence of mind to try to keep her fingers moving before the cold took her. Still, the tips were waxy as I held them.

"She may need more than this." I reached into my jacket and pulled out a credit spike.

I held it out to Bani. "Take this. Find Artin, find a medkit, get some of that soup he makes that she liked so much."

"How much is on it," he asked but didn't hesitate to take the spike from my hand.

"Enough." More than enough, really, but I would use what I needed to get this fixed.

"Does Artin know how to get here with the soup?"

Bani shook his head. "She doesn't like people knowing where she lives. She's had a couple boyfriends here, I think, but otherwise, I don't know of anybody else."

I brushed the lock of hair back from her face, surprised at how much the thought of boyfriends bothered me.

"I'll tell her I had to beat the location out of you, okay?"

"Honestly, I'd rather her be mad at you than me." He headed for the door "I'll be back as soon as I can."

Within seconds, he had done whatever to the door to force it open and then closed it again. Next time I'd have to watch him, have him show me the trick of it. But for now, I didn't really care.

"So cold," Kara murmured, her hand wrapping around my wrist, seeking my body heat.

My shoulders slumped with relief at her words, and I allowed myself the first full breath I'd taken since Bani told me she'd been captured.

I eyed the bed warily. There was no way it would hold both of us. To be honest, it didn't look like I would fit at all, even on my own.

We'd have to make it work. I shifted where I sat on the mattress next to her, then gently lifted her, nestling her upper body against my chest. After swaddling her legs in the blankets, I wrapped my arms around her.

"You're safe now," I murmured. Leaning back against the wall, I rested my cheek against the top of her head and reveled in the feel of her warming, coming back to life.

"And even if you hate me for it, I'll do whatever I need to do to keep you out of danger."

KARA

*M*y dreams were of cold and fire. Cold stealing my breath, taking the movement from my limbs, dragging me into an endless darkness.

Only cold, and pain, and terror.

And then, it was gone.

For the first time since I couldn't remember, I felt safe. Warmth pushed away the last tinges of the nightmare that had held me, but the odd feeling of safety ran through it like threads in a blanket.

I stretched, luxuriating in the feeling. My muscles were stiff, as if I'd been in one position for far too long. Through half-cracked eyelids, I drowsily traced out the secret constellations on my wall, known only to me, since I'd painted the room without reference to any charts.

My breath hitched. What was I doing back home? I'd been out working, looking for something, when...

I shivered, curling in on myself, icy fingers stretching back out of memory to pull me back. My eyes squeezed tight, fighting against it.

"Stop that," rumbled a low voice, so close it startled me despite the quiet tone.

Fully awake now, my eyes flew open. I was home, but, more importantly, why was I lying on top of Davien, and, most importantly of all, why was he in my bed?

His arms tightened around me, and I realized what I thought had been a comfortable blanket over my chest was him. I'd felt safe, and with him. *And we're not going to think about that now,* I decided.

"What's going on?" I managed.

"I don't know, but you got all stiff again. I've been telling you, everything's alright now." He tilted his head to look at me, eyes searching over my face.

I scrubbed at my cheek, unsure of what he was looking for. "I don't remember much, other than the cold."

His lips pressed into a grim line for a flash, so quickly I might have missed it, then softened again. "Not much to remember. Bani saw Sary's soldiers take you. He was smart and came and found me. It's all been taken care of."

My turn to search his face, looking for what exactly he meant by 'taken care of.' Nothing good for Sary's men, I was sure. But how bad? That was an obligation I wasn't sure I could take on.

"I'm sorry, you shouldn't have had to do that, not for me. That wasn't our agreement."

The lines around the corners of his mouth harshened. "What are you talking about?"

"This wasn't related to Helmet Head. Sary's after me for a stupid job that went wrong." He shrugged, as if wanting me to drop it, but I couldn't. I paid my debts. "You shouldn't have had to get involved."

"Figured you're still worth more to me alive."

I laughed, maybe a little shakily, but it was my best effort. "Most folks wouldn't kill to protect their investment. Not such a questionable one, anyway."

He lifted me up just enough to turn me on his lap, facing him. "Who said I killed anyone?"

"Not sure how else you would have convinced Sary to let me go," I half shrugged, not comfortable with any of this.

His lips twitched. "Wouldn't have minded. Not really built to care. But...." What was that expression crossing his face, could it be for the first time since we met, Mr. Arrogant was looking a little sheepish?

"But..." I coaxed.

"I didn't. Just roughed them up some." Of all the things to be embarrassed about, this? "The kid was watching."

I couldn't help it. I laughed at his sour expression. "You pulled your punches because of Bani's delicate sensibilities?"

He shrugged, looking anywhere but at me. "You seem to care about the kid. Didn't know how much you wanted him to see."

Now I was the one embarrassed. "That's sweet. Possibly a bit misguided, but sweet. Mavi's right. You're one of the good ones."

He looked away, obviously uncomfortable.

I lowered my voice. "No, really, you are." Tempted, I leaned forward and brushed my lips against his. "Thanks for rescuing me."

"Always."

A dark hunger underlay that one word, a passion and relentlessness.

His eyes fixed on mine, unreadable. In that moment, the habitual smirk was gone from his lips, replaced by firm resolution. And a promise I didn't understand, but wanted to.

I wrapped my arms around his neck as I darted forward to taste him again, and this time he enveloped me in a crushing embrace.

Heat seared through me, scorching trails left by his hands as they roamed over my back, pulling me even closer. I ran my hands through his short hair, then ran one finger against the edge of a

ELIN WYN

pointed ear. His tongue speared me, and I opened to him without question, moaning against him.

The sound spurred him harder, as his hands ran lower on my back, grabbing my hips, grinding me into him. Through my pants, I could feel the hard length of him, a wave of need clawing through me.

And then I heard a cough from the door.

I froze, and he pulled me to the side of the bed away from the door, twisting his torso between me and any oncoming threat.

But he couldn't block the daggers that went through my heart at Bani's shocked expression.

Bani held a gray insulated bag limply at his side. He shoved it in front of his chest, face wooden. "I got this for you."

I came around the side of the bed, moving slowly, unsure of myself, of him, in this new tension between us.

"Oh, Void, is that from Artin's?"

He didn't answer, just moved around me to put the bag on the desktop, then dug in his pocket for a chip. "He wouldn't take payment." He didn't look around, but put another box beside the chip and the gray bag. "Best I could find at this time of night."

"You did good, kid," Davien answered him, while I just blinked. Obviously, I'd missed a few more things.

But that didn't matter, not now. I wrapped one arm around Bani's stiff shoulders. "Thanks for looking out for me."

He shrugged me off and stepped away. "I didn't do anything. Gotta go."

"You got me food," I tried to keep my tone light. Since when did I care who went where? "Stay and eat at least."

"Nah." He backed away. "Hoyt said he wanted to scout out a place for the littles to crash, figure I'll look him up."

He moved out the door before I could stop him.

Davien squeezed my shoulder. "Eat now. You can fix it tomorrow."

"But…" I sputtered.

"He's had a hard night, too. And now, he went and got you food. You don't want it?"

He moved towards the gray bag and I pulled it away from him. "Mine," I growled.

"That's my girl."

"Fuck you." I peeked in the bag. "There are two servings, actually. Want one?"

"Only if you're sure you won't bite my hand off."

Despite the casual pretense, he dug into the bowl of noodles as if he craved the nutrients as much as I needed the warmth.

For a few moments, I didn't worry about him, about Bani, think about anything other than the spiciness of the broth and the slippery noodles sliding down my throat.

"How did you get Artin to cook so late, anyway?" I threw a glance at the chron near the dresser. "He closed hours ago."

"He was worried, too." Davien looked up over the rim of his bowl, chopsticks still. "You've got a whole bunch of people who care about you, best as I can tell."

Great. More guilt to pile up against the shame of my leaving.

"I know where we need to go to find Helmet Head," I mumbled.

"Tomorrow," was his only answer, between slurps of noodles.

"What?" I asked, bewildered.

"We'll talk about it tomorrow."

"But, don't you want to…."

He shook his head. "Telling me now doesn't do us any good. We're tired, you're healing, we can't do anything about it." He finished off his soup with a slurp. "Tomorrow."

As much as I wanted to talk about our next phase of attack, I couldn't help but agree with him. I wasn't at my best. If I had to plan how we were going to get past two Helmet Heads tonight, I doubted if I'd come up with anything better than sending them invitations to dinner at Artin's, and seeing what happened.

Could they eat through their helmets? They had to take them off sometime, right?

Lost in questions I had no hope of answering, Davien startled me when he stepped away from the desk.

"If you don't mind, I'm going to use your refresher, then hit the sack. We have plenty to plan tomorrow, so stop thinking about it tonight."

The sound of water splashing startled me from the hopeless spiral of thoughts, one crashing into the other.

Even though I had just woken up, weariness from the day ached through my bones.

I tossed our bowls and chopsticks into the recycler to be broken down, then stepped around the half-wall. Davien had set the opacity of the refresher midway; I could make out his broad shoulders, but none of the detail of his hard-muscled body.

Come on, Kara, I chided myself. Weren't you ready to crawl back into bed two minutes ago?

I shook my head to refocus and set the opacity of the rest of the washing station to full.

After I finished my business and brushed my teeth, I thought about the warm shower. I've done a few jobs for the landlord, so my water allowance was a little higher than normal. Still, it wouldn't hurt to double up and save rations, right?

Davien yelped in surprise as I slid in behind him.

"That may be the first completely undignified sound I've heard you make," I said with a grin.

I reached past him for the gel dispenser.

He cocked an eyebrow.

"Are you sure about this? You've had a pretty long day." There's the arrogant bastard I was coming to know so well.

"I am sure...that I want to shower. Everything else is going to have to wait."

I turned away from him and lathered up, reaching for my shoulder blades.

"Here, let me do that. No one can do a decent job washing their own back."

He took the scrubby from my hand and made circles with it on my spine, traveling up and down, back and forth.

"Harder, right there." I arched my spine into the scrubby, bracing my hands against the wall. He'd found an itchy spot.

The scrubbing stopped, and he coughed, then focused his attention on that one spot.

I sagged in relief. "There's nothing worse than having an itch you can't quite reach, right?"

I spun under the water, keeping my eyes averted out of politeness. Mostly. I did take a little peek and darted my eyes away quickly.

Void's sake. Maybe he did have something to be arrogant about.

Before he could catch me looking, I turned him away, back towards the spray of water.

"If I can't reach my own back, there's no way you can scrub all of yours. Give me the scrubby."

I started at the top of his shoulders, working back and forth in small circles, switching directions as I worked my way down the vee of his back to his waist. Nice ass, too.

Possibly the scrubby dipped a little lower on his hip than it should have if I was going to be all business. Possibly.

He turned in my soapy hands so fast I lost my balance, but a firm hand cupped my elbow, keeping me on my feet.

"Keep playing, Kara, and later is going to be now." He growled, sliding one hand around my waist.

I reached behind him to hang the scrubby up, then rested my hands on his shoulders. I tilted my head up to watch him, watch that mouth. Did he realize how much he gave away with those lips?

I licked my own, remembering the taste of him. Dammit, sleep could wait.

Balancing on my toes, I pulled his face down the rest of the way to meet mine.

"Thinking about it again, now sounds fabulous." I reached for him, but he pounced first, hands sliding around my waist, over and under my hips as he lifted me, back against the wall.

My legs wrapped around his waist, arms tangled around his neck, clinging to him, as he devoured my mouth with his own. His tongue demanded entrance, and I opened to him, flicking against him.

He switched his grip to hold me up with one arm, then his hand slid over my breast, kneading, squeezing. I gasped as I slipped against him, and the broad head of his cock nudged against my opening, sending sparks throughout me.

Shuddering, my head fell to his shoulder, eyes closing against the onslaught of sensations.

Tiny bolts of electricity ran from my neck down to my core as he bit and licked his way down my exposed neck. I nuzzled into him, then flicked my tongue over the lobe of his ear, working my way as high up against the pointed rim as I could reach.

He roared, fingers digging into my hip, grinding me into him. Then, when I thought I would shatter, he stopped, panting for air, the cords of his neck straining against an invisible force.

"Don't move."

"Huh?" I blinked, unable to keep up.

He lowered me to my unsteady feet, ran his hands up and down my sides.

"You're going to push me over the edge, and I plan to take my time with you." His eyes ran over my body, and I shuddered from the heat, the desire that touched me as fiercely as his hands.

"What if I want you to fall?" I leaned forward for another kiss, just as the refresher beeped.

"Dammit!"

I pulled him towards me, but not fast enough for us to avoid the freezing spray.

"It's just one of the quirks you get in an older building." I hit the switch to turn the water off. Warm air jetted around us as the drying cycle started.

He glanced around the room. "There seems to be an abundance of...quirks."

"You seem like the kind of guy that can work around surprises," I purred, sliding my hands up his chest.

His scorching kiss was hotter than the drying jets and had parts of me decidedly wet again.

I gave a final spin in front of the hot air, relaxing muscles that had tensed under the sudden onslaught of cold water.

"Get into bed," he whispered in my hair. "I'll be right behind you."

I scampered across the room, the chill in the air sharp against my newly warmed skin.

As I slid between the covers I watched him finishing in the dryer. What was taking him so long, I wondered? His short hair should have been finished in half the time. Of course, I giggled to myself, other parts were considerably bigger.

Suddenly, the room was tinged with the pink glow of the early morning light cycle. I lay stretched out, down the length of his body, his arms wrapped around my back, keeping me pressed against his chest. The room was still mostly dark, only the faintest of street lights shining in from around the window covering.

I pushed up on my elbows to stare accusingly at him. "You let me go to sleep."

In the low light, I could just make out his face. He didn't bother to open his eyes. "You were tired. You didn't complain at the time." He smoothed the hair off my face. "Besides, crushing humiliation is good for me, I'm sure."

"What?"

"You called me an arrogant bastard when I moved you to get into bed."

I scrambled off him, mortified. "I did not," I muttered, as I wrapped the top blanket around me, looking for where he'd put my clothes, and calling for the lights to come back on full.

He pulled on his pants, then padded towards me. "I know there's not a kitchen in your 'quirky' place, but at least tell me you have kaf pods hidden somewhere around here." There was that grin again. "It's the least you can do, after such heartlessness."

I rolled my eyes, then grabbed the mugs and pods from a drawer. "I'm not a complete barbarian."

He pulled the heating tabs on both, then handed my mug back to me as it began to simmer. "But maybe I am."

"Idiot." While the kaf cooled back down to drinkable levels, I called up a line map of the dome on my tablet. "Here," I tapped. "This is the location my friend tracked Helmet Head to."

He flicked the map larger, then toggled the layers to show more detail. "What kind of neighborhood is it?"

I shrugged. "Pretty standard. Not a lot of action, not terribly close to any of the territories. If it's hiding, it's not a bad spot."

Something else tickled in the back of my head, something else important, but a dull headache kept me from grasping it. I rubbed my temple, willing the caffeine to pull it forth, but nothing came.

He tossed back the rest of his kaf, then started dressing. "I'll let you know what I find when I get back."

"Excuse me, what?" I stared at him. "You're not cutting me out of this."

He frowned. "You're not going anywhere. You need to rest."

I stood in front of him, fury blinding me to the ridiculousness of trying to physically stop him.

"You don't own me, no matter what deal you made with Xavis."

His eyes flared wide, then narrowed, jaw tight. "That has nothing to do with this. You could have died yesterday."

"Yeah, I know that. But I didn't. Don't use that as an excuse to control me."

"I'm not trying to control you, I'm trying to keep you safe." His harsh whisper cut sharper than a yell.

"I've been keeping myself safe for my entire life," I bit back, anger burbling the words out faster than I could think. "I don't need you, I don't need anyone."

"Really?" He stalked towards me. I refused to budge, and he bent down over me, hands tight on my shoulders.

"Because yesterday you sure did. You said that little episode wasn't anything to do with me, just previous business. How the hell were you planning to get out of that?

"I…" I didn't have an answer, but he wasn't listening anyway.

"And you needed Bani. And Artin. And weren't you visiting a friend when Sary's men got you?" He kept walking, slowly forcing me to step back until I was flat against the wall, his eyes piercing me. "You have a pack here, friends, people who care about you."

"They don't try to control me," I whispered, unable to look away.

Davien's voice gentled, but his grip didn't loosen. "No, but they want you to be safe."

His lips brushed my temple, hovered by my ear. "And so do I."

His tongue flicked the edge of my ear, and I shuddered in his grasp. He pulled me to him, his lips falling on mine as if he'd devour me, and I clung to him, aching with need.

The sheet fell away as he lifted me, my legs wrapped around him as he walked us back towards the bed, still hungry for each other.

He laid me on the bed, still raining kisses until I was breathless, panting.

Then the bastard spun away, grabbing his jacket and wresting the broken door to my apartment open.

It slammed shut behind him, and metal squealed as he jammed the door.

I banged on the panel, but it wouldn't budge.

"Get some rest, Kara," he laughed. "I'll be back later, and we can pick up where we were."

"Like hell we will!" I shouted at him, trying to rock the now-fixed barrier in its track.

He just laughed again, and I heard his footfalls as he headed down the stairs.

I slid down the door to rest my head on my knees. How could he get me so mixed up, so vulnerable?

And I needed to go with him, because...my brain finally remembered the last piece of information that had eluded me all morning.

Oh, Void.

Davien didn't know there were two Helmets. He might as well be walking into a trap.

DAVIEN

*M*y commlink buzzed again as I strode through the city streets. I didn't bother to look. It'd just be Kara, and I wasn't planning to answer.

She'd called four times already in as many blocks, and whatever she had to yell at me would have to wait until I got back.

Right now, I needed my head back on the mission.

I'd wasted time last night that I should have spent on planning my approach to the Hunter, just lying there, holding her. I shook my head, furious with myself. No wonder the Doc had kept us aboard the *Daedalus*. Spending too much time planet-side, too much time with people outside the Pack, just led to complications. And complications were always best avoided.

Even if they came wrapped up in an intoxicating package of steel and sweetness named Kara.

Maybe especially then.

So, I was going to ignore the scent of her still on my jacket, and catch up on the planning I should have done last night before I got to the address she'd found.

I'd dealt with Hunters, Kara's Helmet Heads, before when they came to the ship, and occasionally, as one of the Pack's first decanted from the growth tanks, sent down on dirt jobs where they were involved.

Didn't know much about them, some sort of modified android was the best guess. Didn't know much about who or what controlled them. Doc said it was some old Empire corp, still running with no one at the controls.

That never quite made sense to me. Doc had some pretty specific supply requirements, and the Hunters were able to get quite a bit, just in exchange for her research data. Someone out there wanted *something* from Doc and wanted it enough to put up with her peculiarities.

But maybe, maybe they'd gotten impatient, a little voice from my gut whispered.

I didn't know who'd attacked the *Daedalus*, didn't think the Doc did, either, before she ordered us into the pods.

But it could have been them...

I stopped, stepped into the shallow recess of a doorway, and ran through some scenarios while watching the street traffic flow by.

If it wasn't the Hunters, their controller might have a way to contact the Doc. That's what I had been betting on since first hearing from Kara that they were here. Even an old protocol would give me a starting place.

If it was the Hunters...

My fist clenched, and I tasted copper. This unit might not have information, but I'd never seen one that wasn't in near constant communications with their organization. The comm restrictions here wouldn't stop Hunter tech, but it'd need some sort of signal booster. And that meant something I could work with.

I nodded and stepped back out, task back in focus.

Either way, I'd get what I needed.

Once at the coordinates, I walked past, just to get a sense of the building. Like everything else in this dome, the squat building had seen better days. Shutters covered the small windows, and I heard nothing within.

Didn't mean anything. Hunters didn't fidget. He, it, whatever, could be in there, just standing still. Or out, doing whatever it was here for.

I walked up to the door, knocked, and listened again.

Nothing.

As far as I understood general rules of etiquette, the polite thing to do would have been to wait, come back another time.

Doc didn't really build us for polite.

Yesterday I was in a hurry. Today, I didn't mind taking a little extra time.

I reached for the seam of the jacket lining. A quick tug opened up one of the hidden pockets and a set of micro tools slid into my hand. Standing by the door, I took a quick look around to see if anyone was near.

The short sequence of sonics triggered automatically when I slid the edge of the card under the plate. A quick green flash and the electronics opened to what it thought was the coded hand-print. Didn't always work, but on any tech older than a year or so, it hadn't let me down.

I stepped inside, then quickly went to the side of the door, taking a quick look around the room while the portal slid shut behind me.

It looked like the rooms had been rented, but Helmet Head hadn't thought much of the furnishings. A small table, a couple of chairs, and a ratty-looking couch were all shoved into the far-right corner. The rest of the room was totally bare. Nothing of the previous resident and nothing that looked like a Hunter had been here. At the back left, a door opened up - another room, a stairway - couldn't tell. I froze, long enough to take a good listen. Still nothing but the soft whine of electronics, so I went to check it out.

As angry as Kara was going to be about me heading out on my

own, I really didn't want to tell her the intel was wrong. I grinned. Or maybe I did. She was kinda fun when she got all riled up...

Dammit, there I went again.

I jabbed a nail into my hand. If I didn't break this habit of letting her randomly into my head, she was going to get me killed.

Back to the mission.

The doorway opened onto a short hall, ending in a flight of stairs. A second door led to another, smaller room.

Jackpot.

Sleek and black, like a cone that flared out in the middle then came to a sharp point at head height, a mini commtower sat in the middle of the floor. A series of slowly blinking lights circled the midpoint. I'd guess they indicated some sort of standby.

Now, decision time.

If I jacked into their communications, it'd be hard to argue I was just stopping by for a friendly visit.

But if I waited for Helmet Head to come back, was I willing to trust its answers about finding Doc?

Fuck that. I trusted Doc, and the Pack, and that was it.

What about... the stupid voice in my head started up again.

I shoved the voice back with a snarl while I sliced open another false seam in the lining of my jacket. A needle slim interceptor. It would pick up anything sent by the tower, and retransmit it to my datapad.

I walked around the commtower, looking for a good place to hide it. Small as it was, it would only work for as long as it remained undiscovered. And having the stupid tower in the middle of the room didn't provide any nice dark corners.

There. One of the lights protruded a fraction of a cen, just enough to lay the interceptor beneath it.

Just in time for me to hear the squeak of the front door.

Maybe, just maybe I could play this both ways.

I walked out of the back room to the front, where the Helmet

Head stood, transfixed, black-uniformed shoulders swiveling as it surveyed the room.

"Hey," I waved casually. "Not sure if we've worked together before, but I heard one of you guys was in town."

It stepped towards me, waiting. Not big on small talk, I guess.

"Anyway, I wondered if you could check with your boss, see if he can get a message to the *Daedalus* for me."

"Information about that project is classified," it answered after a long moment.

I scratched my head. The times I'd worked with one of these, they'd never been big on initiative. But I hadn't thought of it as stupid, either. "Yeah, I'm sure it is. But I'm from the ship. I already know about it. I just want to go home." Sharp pain twisted my gut. Something else the Doc didn't build us for, being away from the Pack for so long.

Another step towards me. "You are from the *Daedalus*," it repeated.

"Just like I said. Doc and your boss can work out the details, we can do another job to make up any expense, but I'm sure she'd appreciate...."

It snagged my arm with a vice-like grip. "You are to be apprehended and returned."

I spun, wrenching my shoulder away from it. "What the hell is your malfunction?"

I backed towards the door. If nothing else, at least one of my questions was answered. The Hunters weren't my allies now, if they ever had been.

Quicker than I thought possible, it moved behind me, blocking the exit. It threw a punch, and with a quick drop I dodged and kicked, knocking it to the ground. But before I could pin it, it rolled and sprung back up like a maniacal child's toy.

As fast as my fists flew, my thoughts were faster. How the hell was this not taking any damage? I grabbed its wrist, spun and twisted it, forcing it to the floor.

It pushed against me, as if it felt no pain at all. Nothing human, nothing at all would have pushed back. I held my grip and gave an additional shove, and it twisted against me, the arm tearing at the shoulder with a sickening rip.

My grip slackened for a moment. Don't blame me. I hadn't expected the ropy mess of flesh tangled with wires that came spilling out of the gash.

It staggered to its feet, off balance by the lack of the arm, but not slowing down. "All results of the Daedalus experiment are to be confined and returned to base." Its voice didn't even sound strained, more like a recording.

There was no way I was going anywhere with that thing. Wasn't happening before, sure wasn't happening now.

The torn arm hung heavy in my hand. Whatever they used to build it was strong, heavy. I shifted the mass, felt for its center of weight, then swung it like a club at the thing's helmet. A satisfying spider web of cracks appeared, and it finally bellowed in rage.

The thing could feel. Either frustration or pain, but an unholy satisfaction bloomed deep within as I pivoted around it, dancing out of the range of its lunges, striking again and again with my improvised weapon.

A chunk shattered, crumbling off the curve of the helmet, leaving a gap no bigger than my fist. Within, a glimpse of fuchsia and magenta intertwined madly. Distracted by the sight, my timing was off just enough that, on the next lunge, it caught my shoulder with a numbing blow. The arm I'd been using as a club spun out of my grasp into the pile of discarded furniture.

"All results of the experiment are to be returned," it repeated, slurring the words now.

"I'd return you myself if I knew where to send you," I backed into the jumbled corner, reaching behind me for anything to use as a weapon. My hand brushed the thin metal leg of a chair. I flexed the metal at the joint. A weak alloy, but it might do what I needed.

I hated relying on 'might.'

It took a lurching step towards me and I sprang, holding the jagged shaft of chair leg in front of me like a short spear. It grabbed me from the air, pulling me in with a crushing grip around my ribs, but right now that suited me fine. I shoved the makeshift spear through the hole in the helmet, stabbing the writhing mass with all my strength, jabbing and grinding while the creature shrieked.

With a final wail, it threw me away. I twisted to hit the wall with my shoulder, and slid down, watching it slowly collapse to the floor. A twitch, another. And then it was still.

I pulled myself to my feet, bracing myself with the wall, keeping my eyes on the wrecked hulk before me.

Damn, that was a lot harder to kill than it should have been. I thought about checking the intercept, but shrugged. There wouldn't be any new comms going out from that thing. With luck, the intercept could pull something out of recent memory and send it to my datapad, but I'd check on it later.

I stretched my side carefully, wincing at the stab of pain from my ribs. At least one had to be broken. I took shallow breaths. Even as fast as I could heal, dealing with a punctured lung would suck.

For now, I needed to find the vials of antonium dust and get back to Kara.

I looked at the remnant of the couch. Kara was pissed, anyway. I should sleep off the worst of it, let my system heal, then search this place.

My head throbbed.

Totally made sense.

Maybe it was just thinking about how many weeks I'd been from the ship, from Doc and the Pack - but I didn't like how long I'd been from her. I straightened up, holding my arm tightly to my side. I'd get her to yell at me later. Find the dust now, get home, then sleep.

Fine. Stupid brain.

Dust wasn't in this room. No place for it in the room for the commtower. So, upstairs it was.

Every ache from the fight kept suggesting I lie down when I went up the first few stairs. Without the Doc and her lab, the only way I was going to heal from this was a long nap. Not here, though.

Halfway up the steps, the front door hissed, and relief ran through me. Wasn't looking forward to the fight with her, but Kara could help search for the antonium, we'd get done faster, and then I could sleep.

Except... The thing on the floor. Tough as she was, that'd freak out anyone. "Hold on, Kara," I called out, turning around to get her. "Right there."

But it wasn't Kara kneeling over the destroyed form.

Damn. There had been two of them.

And I was in no condition to fight.

KARA

*S*tupid jerk.

If he'd waited, if he'd taken me with him, he'd have known what he was getting into.

I called again but didn't expect an answer. I'd be there before the stubborn bastard picked up the comm.

All the time wasted wedging the door open, bit by bit until I could squeeze through the gap.

Void only knew what had happened at those coordinates.

Whatever he'd gotten into, served him right.

I sighed and rolled my eyes at myself. Fine. I didn't really think that. Not after he'd saved me from Sary. And, while I was being honest, he'd saved me back at Xavis', even if I didn't like how he went about it.

But I wasn't going to tell him that.

My stomach growled as I passed another block, further away from the districts I knew best. The coordinates Rati had given me were to a nondescript area, nothing interesting for me. Nothing to steal, nothing to sell. Too quiet.

So why were the Helmet Heads there?

No point in wondering. I rubbed my head from my last

encounter with the weirdo. I just needed to avoid running into another one, find my dust and my guy.

Shit.

I stopped cold in the street, ignoring the mutters of the people who bumped into me.

My guy? Where the hell did that come from?

I didn't have a guy. And if I did, it certainly wouldn't be Davien, with his permanent smirk and know-it-all attitude. Or the way he moved between you and the door, my traitorous brain whispered, or held you all night through the nightmares.

Whatever. I started moving again. He was my partner in this job, my ride off the planet. Nothing else.

I didn't bother going to the front of the building. If Helmet Head came in and out of that door, I didn't want to be anywhere too close. Instead, I walked to the alleyway behind the block, and then counted off buildings. Unlike the center of town, there wasn't much trash in the alley. I examined the wall, searching for handholds. Nothing leaped out as a convenient way up.

There. A thin set of pipes a long-ago resident had run to the roof, three buildings back, no doubt tapping into a water main. I eyed it doubtfully. It was old, but if I moved quickly and carefully, it should hold me all the way to the top.

I slipped on my gloves and flexed my shoulders. Yesterday's adventures weren't exactly the best warm-up for this, but that couldn't be helped. Hand over hand, I moved up the wall, toes braced against the structure for stability, but not much support. The pipe flexed and groaned, but the brackets holding the pipe in place were in better shape than I'd feared.

Only the last gap remained to reach the roof, when, with a groan, the final bracket popped free, and the pipe veered to the side, teetering free of the wall.

Dangling, heart pounding so loud I knew the residents could hear it, I swung my legs back and forth, just a bit, hoping to balance between tearing the rest of the pipe loose, and getting enough momentum to grab the sill.

One, two -- and the next bracket ripped free.

I leaped for it, fingers scrambling, sliding down the wall until I hit a shutter, half knocked loose and hanging from a single hinge.

I clung to it, panting, hand stinging from the fall. Void, anyone in that room would have heard me. I peered between the shutter and the frame and bit back a gasp.

Davien lay on the floor, a bloody mess. No longer caring if anyone heard me, I slammed my fist against the plex. He didn't move, didn't respond.

My heart stopped for a moment, and my head slumped to rest against the glass, eyes closed.

If the Helmet Heads had killed him, I'd find a way to hurt them. Didn't know how, but they walked, and one thing life in Ghelfi taught you was that anyone, everyone, could be made to hurt.

And if he wasn't dead, I'd kill him myself for making me worry.

First step, getting in there.

I rebalanced on the thin window ledge and slid the oxycutter from my jacket. Lightweight and built to fit in my hand, it'd gotten me into more 'unbreakable' buildings than I could count. People focused their security on doors, never thinking to look up.

Never had the cutter seemed so slow, until I finally dropped through the small hole to the floor. I froze, crouched, ready to flee at any noise, but the house was silent.

The air left my lungs in a whoosh as I looked Davien over. One mass of injuries. No one could survive a beating like that. But...

Bands secured his wrists and ankles.

You don't bother to tie up a dead man.

"Hang on, you bastard," I muttered as I bent over his wrists, examining the metal securing him. "I guess it's my turn to play hero."

"Kara?" he whispered. "Get out of here."

"Shut up, you idiot." There wasn't a lock - the metal looked like it had been forged together around him, crisscrossing his wrists. "How the hell do these come off?"

"Don't know. Wasn't awake when they went on."

I glanced at him, half expecting his smirk, but his eyes stayed closed, face still.

"Hey," I brushed my lips lightly over his, careful not to touch anything too hard. "What happened to my favorite smartass?"

He didn't answer, and I returned to figuring out his bonds.

"How'd you get in?" The question was so soft I almost didn't hear it.

"Cutter." Without a lock, there was nothing to pick. And that metal looked a lot harder than plex. Maybe I could find something that could snip it, or force it open, or...

"Then use it again."

I looked at him, shocked. "Can't - no way to angle it without burning you."

"I'll heal." His eyes were open now, expressionless.

I rocked back on my heels, shaking my head. "I've seen people burned from oxycutters. They don't heal." I gripped his hand, desperate for something to hold on to, to ease my panicked breathing. "You can't ask me to do that to you."

He squeezed my fingers back. "Do you trust me?"

I did. Void help me, I did, and I didn't know why. I nodded, unable to speak.

"Then do it. I'll tell you when to stop."

I shook my head, but picked up the cutter.

"Help me sit up, then start there, where it crosses at the top."

No matter how I positioned it, the smell of scorched flesh filled the room.

"Stop."

I almost fumbled the cutter trying to shut it off fast enough.

"You're doing fine, Kara."

I stared at his red, blistering skin. "I can't believe you're telling me it's going to be alright when I'm the one burning you."

He gave a half-laugh. "Believe it or not, I'm feeling a little better than I was. Maybe when we get out of here, I'll take you back home with me, my lucky charm."

"Most folks don't consider being set on fire good luck. You know that, right?"

"What made you think I was most people?" He flexed his shoulders against the wall. "Ready to start again?"

"No." But I did it anyway.

Three more rounds, until the flame of the cutter began to flicker.

"Davien, we may have a problem."

He looked at the small inroads I'd made against the dark metal and shrugged. "Maybe."

He rolled his shoulders, then suddenly swung his arms up, over his head, and around to the side. With a screech, the bands ripped from his wrists, clattering to the sides of the room.

"How did..." I breathed, but he put his hand over my mouth, face intent, eyes distant.

Whatever he listened for didn't arrive, and, after a moment, he moved his hand, brushing my cheek. "Couldn't have done it without a start." He looked at the bands around his ankles. "Think the cutter has enough fuel left to get a nick into that?"

When those scraps had been flung away, more quietly this time, he leaned back against the wall, eyes closed and breathing hard. I looked at his wrists again. Angry red skin, but the blisters had subsided. I examined his face, not shocked now to see the swelling down, the bruising still colorful, but starting to fade.

"What else did you have mod'd?" A memory of water streaming over his hard body in the shower flashed before me. I hadn't noticed anything else but the cosmetic work on the ears and teeth, but this seemed like more than that.

"I didn't do any of it." He slumped against the wall, leaning to one side. "Sorry, still healing." He sagged a little more. "I need to sleep for a bit. You get out the way you came, and I'll follow you as soon as I can."

I snorted. "You can't be trusted to stay out of trouble on your own." I scooted until my back was to the wall. "Come here." I pulled him down until his head rested in my lap. "We'll stay here until you can leave, then figure the next step."

He shook his head, but his movements were sluggish.

"Can you make me leave?" I teased, running my hand through his hair down his shoulders and back.

"Stubborn," he muttered, but closed his eyes again and relaxed onto my legs. I kept stroking his back gently through his jacket. Hopefully, I wasn't hurting him, but unless he said something, I couldn't tell.

I moved from his back to stroke the outer edge of his ear. Such an odd modification, the subtly different shape coming to a sharp point just above the level of his eyes. If his hair was a fraction shorter, there'd be no way to not see it. So why have it done, but keep it mostly hidden?

"Stop that," he murmured.

I froze. "Does it hurt?"

"No. When you do that, all I can think about is burying myself in you until you scream my name."

I choked, face burning. "I see... Does that happen when anyone plays with your ears?"

He snorted softly against my leg. "Nope. Only you."

My mind cast for something, anything to change the subject. "Your ears weren't the only thing changed. What did you mean, you didn't have it done?"

A sigh ran through his body. "That was a stupid thing to say. Any chance you'd forget it?"

"Now?" I touched just the tip of his ear. "Not a chance."

"Fine. How do you define humanity?"

"Well," I blinked. That was a little deeper than I'd been expecting. "Honestly, I'd never thought about it."

"There's a bunch of people back in the Empire who have thought about it, thought about it a lot."

Alright... I wasn't sure where this was taking us, but from the new rigidity of his body, it was important to him. And, surprisingly, that made it important to me.

"One scientist thought their rules and definitions were stupid." A ghost of a smile danced over his lips. "Actually, you'd like her. Neither of you has much use for regulations that don't apply."

I grinned. "You'll have to introduce me sometime."

"I'd like that."

After a long silence, he rolled over onto his back, head still nestled in my lap. I brushed his forehead. "You're stalling, aren't you?"

"I like us how we are," he started.

"Like this?" I snorted. "You beat up, me nearly getting killed yesterday, both of us sneaking around, looking for the dust that weirdo stole from me?"

"No, not that stuff. That's not important." He took my hand and kissed the inside of my wrist, sending lightning through me, and filling my head with thoughts I certainly shouldn't be having about someone hurt as badly as he was. "How we are together." His thumb stroked the back of my hand while he searched for the right words. "We fight, but you hold your own."

"Idiot," I muttered. "I don't hold my own. I fight to win."

"That's what I mean. It feels like partners, like we could be something together." His eyes searched mine. "You're not afraid of me."

His taut face and narrowed eyes would have looked like pain on anyone else. I realized on him, that was worry. I leaned over to kiss him. "I can't imagine anything that would make that happen."

"What do you remember about your parents?"

It was my turn to stiffen. "I don't see why we're going there."

The gentle stroking of his hand relaxed me again. "I remember enough."

He took a deep breath. "I don't remember anything."

"Is that all?" I cupped his cheek. "Half the kids you've seen on the streets here were dumped too young to remember anything. What difference does that make?"

He shook his head. "No, I phrased it badly. I don't remember parents because I don't have any."

I'll admit, my mind had a moment getting around that. "I don't understand."

He pushed himself up until he sat facing me. "I don't have parents because I wasn't born. I was made."

My lack of response seemed to trigger a flow of words, as if waiting for the one thing that would push me away. "My brothers and I were designed, modified in artificial uteruses, then force-grown in training vats. Our cosmetic differences are the smallest changes that the Doc made."

"Someone did this to you...."

"No. I've always been this way. This is all I've ever been, all I've ever known."

My brain stuttered and spun in circles. Right. Answers. More answers would help.

"I have questions."

He nodded, as serious as I'd ever seen him. "Anything."

"Do you kill people for fun?"

"Um... not for fun, I've been on jobs that ended up with people dying." He rubbed his hand through his hair. "I'd guess that most of the time, they were soldiers, too, in someone or another's army."

"Have you ever taken food from anyone?"

An answering frown. "Not really my style, no."

"Ever sold drugs?"

A flat "No."

"Have you ever killed a kid?"

"What?" For the first time, he looked like I'd hurt him.

I forced myself to look into his eyes. "Should be an easy one. Have you ever killed a child?"

"You know me better than that, don't you?" he whispered.

"Well, then," I leaned over to kiss him squarely on the lips. "You're a hell of a lot more human than a lot of people I've met." I looked away, unable to face him with tears in my eyes. "Can we get out of here now?

DAVIEN

*E*very bit of me ached.

I was pretty damn sure a few ribs were still cracked, at the least.

But for the woman who just tossed aside my fear - my entire Pack's greatest fear - and did it with a kiss?

Hell, I'd learn how to fly if she asked me to.

I pushed myself to my feet, fighting to keep any trace of discomfort from my face, and apparently failing.

"Never mind," she tugged my arm. "We should wait, you're still hurting."

"Nope. You're right. We need to get out of here as quickly as possible. I can do it, so I should."

I eyed the door. Helmet Head must have left after tossing me in here. There was no way it wouldn't have heard us. For a thief, Kara had an unusual sense of being quiet.

"I'll go first." I tucked her behind me, and, for a change, she didn't argue, just squeezed my hand and followed.

At the door, I strained my augmented senses to the limit, but picked up nothing but the faint whine of the commtower. "I think it's clear."

In the hall, I paused again, but then she flicked in front of me, through the second and only other door on the landing. "Dammit, Kara," I muttered, but followed her.

Shutters blocked the light from the small room, but it didn't take much to see it was mostly empty, other than a single long crate.

"Locked," she mumbled and patted down her jacket absently, no doubt looking for some sort of pick or breaker.

I glanced over her shoulder for a better look. The crate was made of the same dark, heavy metal that had been used for my bindings, but the hinge had a slightly different sheen to it. Maybe it needed to be softer to swing open. "I don't want us to spend more time here than we need." To be honest, I didn't really care right then why they'd chosen a different metal. I reached over her, shoved my fingers through one hinge, and tore it off, then the other.

"Impressive, but maybe not so bright," Kara observed drily, as I leaned back against the wall, arm pressed tightly into my ribcage.

"Hassle me about it later." I focused on calming my breathing, riding through the pain. "What's in there?"

"Layers of packing foam, so far." Rustling sounds, then a low whistle. "You'd better see this."

I wrapped my arm around her as I came to the side. Partially for stability, sure, but mostly because I couldn't get enough of how it felt when I touched her, like the warm glow of being in the med tank, safe and dreaming.

But what lay in the crate was something out of a nightmare. Long, gray, and gleaming, three long-distance rifles lay like deadly snakes, nestled in their padding.

"What is he doing bringing those here?" Kara breathed. "No one uses firepower like that in the dome."

Unspoken was the fear of everyone who lived here, no matter which side of the law they were on. Just how thin was the dome? What would it take to crack it?

No one knew anymore, the building specifications were long gone. So, other than a few needlers and close-range phasors like Sary had used, there were no guns in the city.

Oddly, it was the packing material that triggered my response. "They came to trade with someone, maybe sell it."

"How do you know?"

Ghost memories of making barricades with discarded sheets of the foam, laughing battles with my pack brothers down the passageways. My throat choked, the words stuck.

"Check the rest of the crate, but the vials aren't here."

She shot me a look filled with the promise of more questions but ran her hands carefully through the rest of the container.

"Nothing. Happy now?"

"Not exactly."

I must have looked as crappy as I felt, because she glanced up at my tone, then blanched. "Shit, I'm sorry. We should get you home where you can rest."

"I'll be fine, but, yeah, I'm ready to go."

She nodded and headed out of the room, moving faster than I expected. I grabbed her before she hit the top stair. "So... you know how you asked about killing people?"

A cocked eyebrow was her only response.

"I'm pretty sure I killed the first Helmet before the second came in."

Her jaw clenched, but she nodded. "I'm glad you landed a few punches first." Her voice was tight under the light tone.

"Hey!" I didn't move from blocking the stair. "The body, it's not like anything I've seen before." Crap. There wasn't a good way to explain this. "I don't want you frightened."

She rolled her eyes. "I thought you were dead. I'm plumb out of freaked for a while." She softened her words with a kiss. "But it's sweet of you to worry."

Intensely aware of her behind me, I moved down the stairs, one cautious step at a time. If I'd misjudged, if the Helmet Head was still down there, I could fight it long enough for her to retreat, get back out through the hole she'd cut in the plex. But I didn't know if I could take it all the way down. My shoulders stiffened. I would just have to do it. No way could I risk it following her.

At the foot of the stairs, I held her back, but still, nothing.

The wall of the front room bore the scars of the two fights. Most of the discarded furniture had been broken past repair, and the dented walls had more than one blood smear.

"Helmet Head," Kara breathed and walked towards the shape on the floor. The second one had moved it to lay against the wall, legs straightened, arm laid over its chest.

The pink tissue entwined with metal had dulled to grey, but the sight was no less disturbing.

Kara slipped her hand into mine. "Ok, maybe I did have a little freak-out left. What the hell is it?"

"I don't know. Doc would. Or, if she didn't, she'd be all over the body, trying to figure it out." Maybe I should try to figure out how to get it back to her. It'd be the favorite gift she'd ever gotten.

"Doc, that's the person that," she paused, and I figured she realized there wasn't a delicate word for it, "made you?"

I nodded, heading for the front door, her hand still engulfed in mine. I decided I liked it there.

We stepped into the street. From the lighting pattern above, it looked it like was still mid-day. Still, no sign of the second Helmet.

"Let's get going while it's good." Kara headed off through the maze of streets. She looked up, a line pressed between her eyebrows. "So, does that sort of make her your Mom?"

I laughed, then apologized quickly. "If what I've seen from old vids on the ship is any indication of motherhood, she's the least maternal person I've ever met. She's just curious about everything."

And I didn't know what was going on. The escape pods

communications didn't have the range to contact the ship, and when I'd gone dirtside before, I'd always had coordinates to meet back up. And I'd never been gone so long. None of us had. When Doc sent us places, it was always in pairs. Hell, some of the younger batches had never even been off the ship.

If the *Daedalus* didn't survive the attack... My throat closed, and I wanted to punch something. Doc would never abandon it, her work, her little empire of science. And my brothers - either dead or scattered among the stars.

With a snap of my attention, I realized I hadn't paid attention to where Kara was taking us.

"Where are we going?"

She looked at me like I'd sprouted another head. "Back to my place. You keep saying you need rest, and it's closer than your room at Xavis'."

"Oh, no, we're not." I turned at the next intersection toward the larger port.

"Fine, Mister Crabby Pants."

"What did you call me?" I glanced down, amused at the nonsense phrase, to see her eyes wide open and staring blindly.

A fast visual sweep of the street didn't reveal any threats.

"Do we need to stop?"

"No," her lips pressed together for a flash, then she grinned with grim resolution. "Why aren't we going home, again?"

"Because it wouldn't be that hard for someone to connect you with me," I turned us again, slowly making our way to the port district. "And while you think you've been careful, nothing is ever as secret as you think."

She threw her hands up. "Then where are you planning for us to go?"

I grinned, glad she'd been distracted. "Waiting for you to tell me."

"You're impossible, you know that, right?" She moved as if she were going to storm off, but I pulled her back to me with a light tug.

"Quick, name the three fanciest dormers at the port?"

"You're kidding. We don't have the credits to spend on a bunk rack like that." Her eyes narrowed. "Do we?"

"Come on, come on." I snapped my fingers, knowing it would just piss her off.

"Fine." She rolled her eyes. "The Polaris, the Rings, and Meshato."

"Great. Now, name the three sleaziest."

She socked my shoulder. "How do you think I'd know that?" A quick glance, and a smile. "Anything Xavis owns. So, the Lux, the Cisytem, and the Shaft. Oh, the Merryden should be in there, too."

I kept us walking, looking around for anyone that looked too interested in us. Nothing yet, but I didn't want to be on the street too much longer until I was back at full strength. "Last question."

Kara laughed. "I doubt it, but sure, go ahead."

"Three more dormers."

"This is a stupid game, you know that?" But she looked distant, in thought. "Well, there's the Fujara and the Star." We waited for a food cart to pass us, the fragrant steam making my stomach rumble. "Oh, and the Imperial. I always forget that one."

"Then that's where we're going. If it's the last place that comes to your mind, that'd be the last place someone would look for you."

She looked up at me, either doubt or amusement in her eyes. Maybe both. "That makes a certain crazy sense. But, just so you know, the Imperial isn't nearly as grand as it sounds. It's right on the edge of the dome, and entirely run by bots."

"Sounds perfect." My stomach rumbled again, loud enough to hear over traffic. "Just as long as we can get food there."

"It won't be like Artin's," she said, sadly.

"Nope. But I hate to tell you, not many dinners in the 'verse are like his. Better get used to disappointment."

The dormer was everything she promised. Small, a little rundown, too far out of the way of the path of most travelers to be convenient, not cushy enough to be worth the extra blocks for the rest.

I used a scrap of my shirt as a makeshift glove while flipping through rooms on the display. It wouldn't be hard, if someone knew what they were doing, to pull my print from my doorlock at Xavis', and run a match search for any other prints.

The rooms weren't as bad as the location made out, if outrageously priced. Kara gasped when I slipped a credit spike in after selecting the best thing offered.

"That's a ridiculous amount for a bed."

"Nope. Totally reasonable." I watched the lights flicker on the spike. In theory, it should rotate through account data, making it hard to track us by purchases. But I hated trusting the tech. "It's not just a bed, it's a bed big enough to fit me. And the best-stocked replicator they have. And a shower." I waggled my eyebrows at her until she laughed.

"Food first," she pushed me towards the waiting lift tube. "Then a nap."

"And then?" I followed her inside, wrapping my arms around her.

She stood on her toes, her lips against mine a promise. "Then, we'll see."

I wasn't the only one hungry. Almost before I got the door open, Kara had dashed to the replicator. "What do you want?" she called over her shoulder as she flipped through options.

"Anything." I tossed my jacket to the bed and eased into a low-slung chair, a choice I'd likely regret when I needed to get out of it, but it looked comfortable now. "Actually, anything with lots of protein."

I closed my eyes, must have drifted for a few minutes, because Kara stood beside the chair, stroking my forehead. "Dinner's ready," she said. "Want to come to the table, or try to eat here?"

I reached to lift her over the arm of the chair. "Ten more minutes," I answered, nestling her down onto my chest, wrapping my arms around her. "Promise I'll get up then."

"Sure you will." She kissed my cheek and threw one arm around my neck as she snuggled in. "Good thing I left the food in the warmer."

We hadn't opened the window seals when we came in, so I didn't know how long we slept, but it wasn't ten minutes. I ran through a quick self-diagnostic, flexing individual muscles, checking for residual pain and strain. Not one hundred percent yet, but closer than I would have expected.

Kara must have been just as exhausted, she'd rolled slightly so her face was buried in my shirt, but otherwise hadn't moved. I listened to her even breathing, her own calm spreading through me like a soothing balm.

Then a thought hit me, harder than one of Helmet Head's punches.

My arms must have tensed, because Kara pushed away from my chest to brush the sleep from her eyes. "What's wrong?"

"You can't come with me," I blurted.

Her eyes narrowed, but she didn't answer, just wiggled off me and the chair and headed towards the corner with the table and the replicator.

"Come have lunch."

I pushed out of the chair, trailing her, the rest of my mind a whirl around the one, clear thing. "I'm sorry, but I can't take you. I'll get you money, get you and Bani and Artin and whoever you want passage anywhere you want, but-"

She placed covered bowls from the warmer on the table, arranged them just so, then went back for another plate. The only indication she'd heard me at all was the stiffness of her spine.

"You've obviously had your head hit too many times. You should eat."

When I didn't move, she sat. "I'm hungry, at least."

I sat down, uncovered my bowl. My stomach grumbled again at the spicy scent of the thick stew, but I just stared across the table, willing her to let me explain.

"I knew you were hungry. We probably should have gotten something in you before the nap. Who knows how much that healing takes out of you," she commented mildly, as she took a small bite. "Not bad, really." Her eyes flicked up, met mine, daring me to break the temporary illusion of normalcy.

"Um." My spoon hovered over the bowl, remembering lectures from shipboard. "A lot, actually. Doc had charts about what nutrients we needed to replace for each level of damage before our systems start cannibalizing themselves and making things worse. Usually, we just carry nutribars to keep stuff topped off until we get back to the medbay."

Kara blinked. Dammit, maybe that wasn't the right answer. I had no idea how to play this game.

She took a sip from her glass. Lips pursed, she put it down quickly.

"What's wrong?" I sniffed the orange stuff filling my own cup. Both sweet and tart, it was strange, but not unpleasant.

She looked at her glass sadly. "Orange juice. I couldn't believe they had it on the replicator menu. I had it once, and it was fantastic. I wanted you to try it."

I sipped my glass, cautiously. The taste was strong but good. But after a taste of the stew, I knew what was wrong.

"The juice is fine, it's great, actually." I went to the replicator and dialed up two glasses of red wine. I was going to need it. "It just doesn't go with the stew. It's not the right time for it."

I took a long drink of the wine, the heavy tang washing away the sweetness of the juice. "It's sort of like us."

She took a sip from the wine glass. "You're right, this is better."

"Kara, we can't stay together. Right now, we're like the stew and the orange juice." Damn it, that made no sense.

At least it caught her attention, got past the shell she'd put up.

"Interesting. What do you mean? We work great together. And, I thought..." She looked away.

"Void." I knelt by her chair, wanting to cup her face, soothe away the hurt in her eyes, but I kept my hands safely to myself. "We both thought. But the timing is wrong."

She looked at me blankly, then pushed away from the table, away from me. "I'm getting a shower."

I watched her peel out of her clothes, long legs for her small body. Lean, less from toning and vanity, probably more from never enough to eat, and having to wiggle into tight places for her work.

My eyes wandered down the length and curves of her. She was going to kill me. Just being around her, I could taste the scent of her in the air, crushing my resolve.

"Kara, we are good together."

She stepped into the refresher, turned on the water, and closed the door. "You'll have to speak up."

I moved closer to the refresher but kept my eyes fixed on the ceiling. At least, I tried to, but I couldn't help but watch her as she stood under the water, her hair slicked away from her face. Even under the massaging pulses, her shoulders were stiff.

Waiting for me to deliver the blow.

"Kara, you've got to understand. I didn't know. But it looks like my people, the Doc and the Pack, are at war with the Helmet Heads. And I don't know how many there are."

I slumped against the wall.

"I don't want you in the middle of it. I don't know if I can keep you safe."

She flung open the shower door, ignoring the water spraying on the floor around her.

"I never asked you to keep me safe. I didn't think that's what we were basing this…" she waved wildly "whatever the hell it is between us on."

Kara continued, and I backed away from the fury in her eyes.

"Who the hell are you to talk about trying to keep me safe? Who was keeping you safe earlier today? What, exactly, were you going to do if I hadn't come around, looking out for your ass?"

I pushed back towards her, my own anger riled. "I would've healed in time. I needed to rest and then I would've gotten out on my own just fine, thank you."

She dried off quickly. "Sure you would've. It looked like you were doing a great job of that."

I moved to grab her arm, but she stalked away, snatching her clothes up from the floor. "You know," I yelled, "it might have been easier if I had known that there were two of them at that address."

"And who's fault is it that you didn't," she spat back, toweling her hair. "You're the one that left me behind, didn't give me a chance to tell you."

I ran my hand through my own hair, to keep my hands busy, to keep from ripping the leggings and shirt out of her hands, rather than let her keep dressing. "Don't go."

"Fuck you," she shrugged on her jacket. "You can't have it both ways."

"You're not safe here."

"Not your call." she tugged on her boots and moved towards the door.

"No," I growled, grabbing her and spinning her towards me.

"You can't have it both ways, Davien." The hint of tears glistening in her eyes cut me more than her words. "You either need me, or you don't."

I buried my face in her hair. "Void forgive me, I need you."

Kara tugged my shirt front impatiently, pulling me towards her. "Then do something about it, why don't you?" she whispered, then kissed me. There was nothing gentle in her touch this time, only hot fire and desire. Like molten ore burning through a reactor wall, every desire I'd had for her broke free at her kiss. I pulled her to me, cradling her head with one hand while fighting with the clasp of her shirt with the other.

"Why the hell did you put on clothes?" I muttered while pulling it off her shoulders.

"Because you were being a dick," she answered, pressing against me, her hands running under my shirt, brushing the waistband of my pants. "Besides, you're still dressed, too."

I stepped away long enough to pull my shirt off, and returned to kissing down her neck, craving the taste of her. "You've got to get out of your pants now," I growled. "I don't think the replicator here is programmed for clothing."

She pushed me back against the wall, and I waited, nearly panting with need for her, while she kicked off the boots and wiggled out of the stupid pants.

In seconds, she was back, her skin pressed against mine, arms wrapped around my neck. My cock strained painfully against its confinement. "I like those pants," she murmured, then nipped at the edge of my ear.

Void, if she did that again, I'd need new clothes myself.

With a growl, I picked her up, and, with two long strides, took her to the bed. "We've got to talk about things, Kara."

She slid out of my arms to kneel on the bed, her hands busy at the fastenings at my waist. She stopped, then stroked my straining length through the fabric.

I groaned, knees buckling, and she grinned. "Now, or later?"

I tore off the pants, seams be damned, and forced her back to lay on the bed.

"Later."

She pulled me towards her as she lay back, but I was done being led. I had other plans. I lay outstretched next to her. "Hold still, sweetheart."

"What?"

I pinned her wrists above her head with one hand and, with the other, palmed her breast, feeling her nipple harden at my touch. "For once in your life, would it kill you to listen to me?" I fell on her lips, drinking in the feel of her writhing beneath me, the softness of her skin. My hand slid lower, and I rubbed two fingers at the v of her legs.

"Oh, Darkness, Kara, you're so fucking wet," I mumbled into her neck, then swallowed her scream with my mouth as one finger slid inside her, followed by a second, slowly pumping. I ground the heel of my palm onto her mound and, as if lit on fire, she arched up, shattering around me.

As her breathing slowed, I rolled onto her, raining kisses down her neck. "I can't hold out anymore, Kara," I growled.

She wrapped her legs around my back, guiding me towards her. "I never asked you to."

Her nails bit into my shoulder as she pulled, and, with a shout I, rammed into her.

From that moment there was nothing else, nothing but her beneath me, my pounding into her, her legs tangled with mine, the taste of her sweat and her soft cries, the feel of her heat encasing me, the sound of my pulse rising higher and higher until, at one hard thrust, she screamed "Davien!" and I roared, losing myself into her in a shudder of release.

KARA

*S*lowly, I pulled myself back together, my scattered thoughts returning to my still throbbing body.

Davien rested on his elbows above me, head dropped down onto my shoulder, panting. I ran one hand down his back and he turned his face to nuzzle my neck.

"That's not what I meant to do," he moved to hover over me, his face inches from mine, his eyes scanning over me.

I mustered the strength to give a little squeeze down below and he yelped.

"I don't remember objecting." The words flashed me back to how we met, to struggling beneath him in his quarters when he proposed working together. Months, years ago, surely. I couldn't feel this way about someone after only a few days, could I?

His hands on my skin pulled me from my thoughts, left space for nothing else but sensation.

"This time," he said stroking my hair back from my face, punctuating his words with kisses and nips, "this time, I'm willing to take my time and enjoy you."

And he did. And I did.

Afterwards, I lay tangled in his arms, half sprawled over him, legs intertwined with his.

He pulled the covers up over us both and I nestled into his shoulder.

"We're going to have to talk about some things, Kara" he started.

"Later," I mumbled and kissed his chest before drifting off to exhausted slumber.

An unknown time later, my eyes flew open, heart pounding from dreams of running, scared and hungry, through the streets of the city.

Davien rolled over and tightened his arm around me, but didn't wake.

What the hell was I doing here?

He seemed like a good guy. I wasn't enough of a liar to deny there was something between us, and, Void take me, the sex was hot. But he was caught up in some mystery. It wasn't that I minded the danger, but I couldn't be kept in the dark.

I refused to be lied to. Not again.

The lights switched to nighttime patterns as I stared into the room. There wasn't a good decision here. Sure, maybe he could get me off-planet. But at what price? I could feel myself edging towards feelings for him that I thought were damn near buried. And they certainly weren't appropriate if he wasn't going to be telling me the truth.

No. This had to end now. For just another moment I lay there, safely enclosed in his arms, wrapped in the spicy scent of him and listening to his heartbeat.

Then I began to slowly slide out towards the edge of the bed. I sat up and swung my feet to the side when suddenly his hand was around my wrist.

"You were right." His voice was so low I almost couldn't make out the words.

"What?"

"I didn't ask what you wanted. Didn't ask if you needed to be kept safe." He sat up and wrapped his arms around me from behind. "I'm sorry. I never thought of myself as stupid, but you make me kind of dumb that way."

I leaned back into him. "Tell me," I said, leaning back into him. "Tell me everything that's going on."

A deep sigh. "That's part of the problem. I don't know, either. Something's wrong." He started over. "I already told you the Doc created me, well, me and the rest of my brothers."

I nodded. I knew, which wasn't quite the same as understanding or having my head wrapped around it. But, well, it was a big strange universe and I was pretty sure this wasn't the strangest thing out there.

"The Doc was always working on possible improvements for new batches, new enhancements. Along the way, she had contact with a lot of pretty crazy people. And, of course, all of this was expensive. The Helmet Heads were couriers between her and someone else. Sometimes we worked with them, but usually they just came and went with supplies."

He paused. I couldn't see him but, leaning against his chest, I could feel the emotions running through him.

I squeezed his arm. "Something happened. You're worried about her."

"She got a private comm, scrambled. And, whatever it was, she told us all to get in the pods, to get away and wait for orders. We all did, except for the few that were still in the batch tanks, or in the lab for mods and checkups."

I waited, listening to his breathing shift, get shallow, tight.

"The ship has some defenses, but it's a floating lab, not a warship. Still, it never occurred to me that she needed us." He gave a little laugh. "I've never seen anything she couldn't talk her way out of."

He stopped laughing, all traces of lightness gone. "We jumped, scattered, just like she said. And I lost track of all my brothers, and the ship."

"And you don't know who messaged her?" I whispered. He'd lost his home, his family, the woman who may not have been his mother, but was the closest he would've had. No wonder he was a little on edge some of the time. Well, most of the time. Dealing with the mental fallout from my family situation still made me want to punch something occasionally, and that was old news.

"I didn't, but when I was fighting the Helmet Head, he kept talking about the results of the Daedalus experiment being brought back to base."

I turned around to face him. In the half-light, I could see his strong cheekbones, the shape of his face, but not much else. "Base?" I asked. "Whose base? And where?"

He shook his head. "No idea. But I have a lot more to do than just waiting for orders. I'd already planned to get out there, find the *Daedalus*, find my brothers." His voice hardened. "And now I'm going to find that base and destroy it."

I thought for a few long moments. But really, the answer seemed clear.

"Then we better get busy getting us a ship. None of those things are going to happen while we're stuck here."

His arms squeezed so tight I almost couldn't breathe. "Are you certain? This isn't your fight."

I tilted my head up and kissed the line of his jaw. "It is now."

Davien's shoulders sagged as if he'd been tensed for a blow, and now all the waiting was over. Still, he didn't release me. "Good, because I wasn't sure if I was really going to be able to let you go."

Words bubbled up in my throat, but I couldn't risk saying them, not yet. Safest to keep my thoughts on task. "First order of business should be to actually get a meal in us, get showered, and have a proper night's sleep. And then we can start in the morning."

Davien's eyebrow rose and that stupid smirk I was beginning

to fall a little in love with was back on his face. "And where do you think we can go from there?"

He rolled with me in his arms back onto the bed, twisting until I was beneath him. "I took you from his office because I thought I was saving you." He kissed me long and deep. "I think I was saving myself."

Eventually, we did get dinner.

In the morning, I pulled my clothes out of the closet aerator and gave them a quick sniff. Not the best job in the world, and not my preferred cleaning insert. But it would certainly do.

"You don't think Helmet Head's going back to the same house, do you?" Davien asked.

"No idea. But I know who can find him again. We don't have enough time to search the entire city. You've got things to do, right?"

"Where we're going today," I paused, shrugging on my jacket. "It's probably best if you don't ask too many questions. She's not terribly social."

"Like you?" Davien handed me a glass of orange juice and a completely inappropriate burst of happiness spread through me. Even from the middle of our fight, he had remembered.

I took a sip while he finished dressing. "Think we'll come back here?" I asked. It wasn't a fantastic room, but I felt like my entire life had changed within its slightly rundown walls. I shook my head. Since when did I get so sentimental?

Davien stood behind me and flicked my hair out of the way to rub my shoulders. I leaned back into him. Oh yeah. Since this.

"If that's what you want. You know, there's an entire universe out there of things I can't wait to show you." He kissed the top of my head, then wisely stepped out of reach. "But, if you have a preference for third-rate racks on fourth-rate planets, I'll see what I can do to oblige."

"Jerk."

I downed the last of the orange juice and put the glass in the recycler to be broken down for whoever stayed here next.

"Come on, smartass. Let's go meet Rati."

The bunk rack where we'd ended up was clear on the other side of the dome from Rati's quarter. Even though I usually hated taking it, the tram would be the fastest way to get there.

We hopped on one of the branch lines. I usually avoided the eyes of all the citizens who kept their heads down, kept working, and had no idea of the secret wars between the coalitions happening in the city. Their world always seemed so different, so remote from mine.

But this morning I let my mind wander, thought about the people who just lived here, worked, lived out their lives, and weren't involved in the brutality underpinning it all.

I stole another glance, eyes moving from one face to another.

They looked tired, some of them, but it was morning and they were headed off to work or to catch another roller out to one of the mining camps, or wherever.

Hell, I should be tired after our time 'resting.' A smile crept across my face and I kept looking at the passengers, imagining where they might be going, what their lives might be like.

And then I blinked.

At the front of the tram, I caught a profile I recognized.

I squeezed Davien's hand. He looked down, and I was tickled to see the slight smile on his lips matched how I felt.

"At the front of the compartment, blue shirt, high collar." I turned my eyes back to the interesting person. "Tell me who you think that looks like."

He flicked his eyes for just a moment and then looked away. "The kid who takes care of the littles in the stairwell."

I nodded. "Hoyt. I thought so."

Davien looked down, brow wrinkled. "Any reason he shouldn't be on the tram? I mean, we are."

I shook my head. "No," I dragged the word out, thinking. "But something feels off. It seems early for errands. I don't know, it's probably nothing."

Davien watched the front of the compartment for a few moments longer. "I think you're right. His stance is braced, nervous as if he's anticipating something. There's something going on."

I made a fast decision. "Let's follow him, at least for a bit." We were almost to where we would have to get off, anyway. I thought about the time. And Rati probably wouldn't mind having callers slightly later in the day.

Davien nodded. "I 'hired' you for your local knowledge. If you think something's wrong, I'd rather find out sooner than when it blows up and knocks our plans off course with it."

Hoyt got off the tram two stops later. He looked around, but we hung back before jumping off the back of the tram at the last minute. Delaying meant we nearly lost him as he went inside a dive bar, one of the greasy kind that made me squirm.

If you never closed, when the hell did you clean? And, from the times I'd been on a job and in one of those places, there was lots to clean.

"Is he old enough to go in there?" Davien muttered.

I stared at him, shocked speechless.

"Right." He smirked. "Really the question is, when is it too early for a drink?"

I shook my head and made a slow stroll across the street. A quick glance was enough to show me Hoyt seated at a table at the back, talking urgently with another person. The stranger kept to the shadow of the booth, making it hard to recognize him.

"Shall we?" I slipped my hand into the crook of Davien's arm, and we headed in.

"I'm not sure we'll be having the orange juice here," he commented when a robot attendant rolled forward. No vocals, nothing other than a limited selection of liquids from the house replicator. Davien poked two things at random and paid.

"I know, I didn't ask you," he said as we slid into a booth across the room. "But only because I'm sure you wouldn't actually drink anything here. Think of it as table rent."

If nothing else, the drinks were cold. I kept my hands on the glass, figuring if the container was freshly recycled, it was likely the cleanest thing in the room.

The guy Hoyt was talking with kept twitching, looking around in a short pattern, then head back down. His face was half-covered by a mask, and there was something odd about his jacket. He kept his hood pulled up, nothing too unusual, but the pattern all over was strange, blocky, disturbing. I'd seen him before, somewhere, but the memory stayed just a tickle.

"Face duplication camo," Davien said, putting down his glass after a short sip. "Don't scrunch your face up. It's not that bad." But I noticed he didn't drink again. "The pattern on the fabric has all the identifiers that face recognition software searches for - something that looks like eyes, nose, and so on - but repeated over and over, slightly distorted. Low tech, but throws the systems for a loop, even makes it hard for human eyes to match it with someone they know well."

"I guess..." I trailed off, still trying to place the guy. "But couldn't you just program the system to track anomalies, and then re-filter on them?"

"Only if you're smarter than your average despot," Davien grinned. "Whoops. I think we've been noticed."

I glanced back over, and Hoyt and his friend were bent over the table, whispering furiously and shooting us dark looks. Suddenly, the other man stood up, pulled the mask to cover his entire face, and stalked away.

"Scum," he muttered as he passed our table.

Davien bristled, but the voice had triggered another memory. Waiting in a bar not unlike this, getting a handle on my mark, his daily patterns. There had been a table nearby, people talking loudly about something. Emotions had run high, voices loud with lots of hand waving. Most of the guys there had been in similar jackets and masks. But this guy, I knew him from somewhere else, I was sure.

Hoyt walked up, anger rolling off him, eyes blazing at Davien. "Have I been targeted now, enforcer?"

"Good morning to you, too," I answered.

Since when had Hoyt looked at me like I was the enemy?

"Why are you following me?" he snapped back.

"Believe it or not, I have business in this quarter that has nothing to you with you." Mostly. Rati was in the quarter, so that made it not quite a lie, right?

His defenses started to slide down, then Davien spoke.

"Who was your friend?"

"None of your business. Don't you have errands to run for Xavis?"

Davien ignored the implied insult. "Last time I checked, happy people didn't usually wear optical camo. Makes folks think you've got something to hide."

The topic of the overheard conversation from months ago came back to me with a jolt. "He's part of the Bedrock Core, isn't he?"

Hoyt looked away, and my stomach plummeted.

"Hoyt, they're just another gang. No one wants a war."

"It's not a gang," he muttered. "We're going to stop the gangs, get rid of them."

I shook my head. "I've seen what happens when people go against Xavis. There's no way out, once you're in, unless it's through the airlock to the Waste."

Hoyt sneered. "I would have thought you'd be the last person to defend Xavis."

I tried my final card to break through. "What about the kids? If there's an attack on the complex, how are you going to keep them safe?"

A flicker crossed his face. "We're moving them today. It's a crappy way to live, always underfoot."

I remembered what Bani had said when he'd brought soup to my apartment, what felt like lifetimes ago. "Is Bani helping you?" A knife twisted, cold in my guts. "Hoyt, he's too young to get caught up in this."

"He's old enough to make his own choices, just like any of us." But he softened. "I just have him cleaning up some space at the old refinery. Not much harm can happen to him there."

I stood up and Davien rose, towering over us both. Hoyt stood his ground. "Hoyt, I don't know what you think, and I don't want to tell you what to do." I stuck my hand out. "But thanks for keeping Bani and the littles out of it."

After a minute he responded, his handshake more that of a man's than the boy I'd taken him for. "Check for Bani at the top level. He's probably still there, if you want to find him."

As we stepped out of the dive, I was torn. The old refinery was back the way we'd come, in a completely different quadrant. We should get to Rati's first, find out what she could help us with, get her started on whatever searches we needed.

Davien had already headed down the walkway. "Aren't you coming? I thought the refinery was this way?"

I hurried to catch up. "Don't you think we should talk to Rati first?"

He shook his head. "I'd rather round him up before whatever your little friend is planning hits the street. Better than wasting time looking for him when we're ready to get off-planet."

"Besides," his voice softened, "I don't think you got a chance to catch up with him yesterday, straighten things out. That's on me."

"Idiot." I wrapped my fingers around his hand as we caught the next passing tram, gliding along towards the northern sector.

Once upon a time, when the city was built, the plan was that robots would do the mining, and automated roller wagons would bring the raw ore in for sorting and refinement.

Maybe that worked while the Empire was still in charge, but

no one had the money to repair the old droids, much less replace them. Humans were cheaper, and could be talked into doing all sorts of crazy things for the chance of a big payoff.

The rollers had been modified into carriers for the miners, and refinery operations had been moved to a series of mobile buildings in the Waste. As mining operations moved, so did they.

The system worked as well as anything else in Ghelfi, but once the warehouses had been torn down, it left the control center standing alone, a tall, narrow building that did no one any good.

Unlike most buildings, no one squatted there - too many old machines and terminals crammed into the rooms to be normal family housing. But for a group of kids used to hiding in back alleys and stairwells, it would be heaven.

Just like Hoyt had promised, it didn't take long to find a tousled dark head poking around the wiring, shoving components to the side to clear paths.

"Here, let me help." I bent down to put my shoulder to the crate he was straining against, and he jerked away.

I stood and stepped back, more hurt than I thought I'd be. "Bani, what's going on?"

He shot a dark look at Davien, who'd had the sense to stay back, leaning against the wall, looking for all the world as if he just happened to be there.

My face flushed. "I didn't mean for you to walk in when you did. But even still," I ran a hand through my hair. "Kiddo, you know I've had boyfriends. You knew Juda. You never had a problem then."

He scowled and looked away. "I thought you were hurt. I was worried about you, and I got back and you were fine." He spat out the last word as if it were poison in his mouth. "You said you'd come by yesterday."

"Things got crazy with a job." Which was sort of the truth. Sort of.

"You spent it with him, didn't you?"

"I thought you liked Davien? At least well enough to find him when I needed help."

"Yeah, he was good for that. But I didn't think you'd be like this."

"Like what?"

He shrugged and turned away.

"Bani," I reached for his shoulder. "I'm trying to get us off-world, wouldn't you like that? A better city to live in, no worrying about the tithe, or anyone being thrown into the Waste?"

He tore his arm away, took a step back with his eyes wide. "Did you ever even ask me if I wanted to leave?" He shook his head slowly. "This is my home. My friends are here." He looked at Davien and his eyes narrowed "It's him, isn't it?"

I let out a breath slowly. "He needed some help, and we worked out a deal."

Bani's lips twisted into a sneer. "Everyone was right. You're a whore, just like your mother."

His words slapped me, harder than an actual punch would have. I couldn't say anything, couldn't even breathe. In a blink, Davien stood between me and Bani, large hand gripping the front of Bani's thin jacket.

"Apologize," he growled.

I looked past him at Bani's face, pale with fear. And something else flickered behind his eyes. Regret. He needed space, he lashed out the only way he could.

"Put him down, Davien."

"He needs to learn some manners."

I laughed, maybe a little shakily, but it was the best I was going to do right then. "I'm pretty sure we all do." I touched his shoulder, dropped my forehead to rest on his back, breathing in the solidity of him. "Let's go. We've got things to do."

We left the refinery without another word. When I glanced behind us, I could see Bani's face through one of the upper windows, hand pressed to the plex.

DAVIEN

$\mathcal{I}$ fought the anger back, forced myself to walk normally. "Which tram now?"

Kara shook her head, eyes still wounded from Bani's words. "I'd rather walk, if you don't mind."

We headed through the streets, the silence pressing. Enough. "So... want to pick a different passenger to come with us?"

She smiled, but it was tight, a mask only. "Nah. Kids say stupid stuff sometimes, you know?"

I shook my head. "Actually, I don't. By the time we were decanted, we'd had so much training piped into us, I doubt if we acted much like normal kids."

Kara looked up, rolled her eyes. "Didn't you get into trouble at all?"

"Sure, there's never too many in one batch, but Doc probably brought out about three to five of us a solar. So sometimes it must have felt like whole mobs of teenaged boys roaming the ship, all of us stir-crazy, reckless, and trained for action. One cycle, we were so wild she forbade us entry to the labs, but it didn't take long before we bypassed the system, thought we could make our own improvements."

I couldn't help grinning at the memory. "Turns out she'd been watching us from control, and had a fine time shutting off the lasers every time we got ready to use them. They'd be working one minute, then poof! No power the next."

"So... Lasers, yes, but you never sassed?" Kara asked, finally rewarding the ridiculous but true story with a real smile. I searched my brain for other glimpses of shipboard life that might amuse her.

"Well," I blushed. "Maybe for sassing occasionally. There may have been times she threatened to space the lot of us and start over."

But that was more than just sass, I thought. That meant to hurt you, and it did. The anger ran through me again, just as hot.

We continued until she broke the silence. "My mother never threatened to throw me out the airlock, at least. I guess here it would be to toss me into the Waste. She hung on me, wept, apologized."

"Apologized for what?"

"Everything. For failing. For getting addicted. For having me."

I wanted to pick her up, tuck her away, but she kept walking next to me, eyes fixed forward. I took her hand and squeezed it, the only comfort she'd let me give her right now.

"She was a scientist. I found the record chips when I was a kid, searching for credits. A geologist, here from someplace further towards the Imperial hub. She'd come out to study the rock formations. Apparently, antonium is rare enough everywhere else that someone thought it might be worth the investment to see if it can be artificially created."

I stayed silent, waiting, but my thoughts raced. An improbable experiment, but one Doc Lyall would have approved of, even if it wasn't her field. Antonium was the final component in modern star drives. An artificial source could change the economy of the entire Empire.

Kara's eyes were so lost in the past, I couldn't help but wrap my arm around her, tug her off the street into a quiet alley.

"What are you doing? We need to get to Rati."

"Rati will wait." I kissed her, long and deep. "Come back to me, Kara. Wherever you are, it's not real, not anymore."

She leaned into me, and I held her, itching for something solid to fight. Memories were too sneaky of a target, even for me.

When she started talking again, her voice was muffled by my jacket, too low for human ears. That was fine. I was built for this.

"Maybe she was having trouble with her research. Maybe she was just stupid. But she got started on Purity. Said it helped her focus." Kara sagged against me. "After a while, she needed something else to let her sleep. And before she knew it, all her grant money was gone, and she'd hocked her ticket home for another hit."

Her voice dropped even lower. "Apparently there wasn't a lot of jobs for a constantly drugged-out research geologist. So, she did what she could to keep the money and drugs flowing. And when even those jobs dried up, she whored for it. Mix up enough Rabbit with Serenity, and she didn't even care."

"And you?" I whispered, matching my voice to hers.

"Apparently, if you're high all the time, it's easy to forget to have your implant renewed. I was a bit of a surprise. At first a welcome one, she thought motherhood would be like having a doll, something that would always love her, never question."

"Your father?" Surely someone would have taken pity on her, kept her safe.

A bitter laugh. "My mother and Xavis had an arrangement, but it wasn't exclusive, just her tithe. I've refused a DNA scan. If I really have his genes in me, I don't want to know."

The sounds of the city around us faded away, she was lost in the past, and I wanted to be there with her, somehow shielding child-Kara from the ghosts that even now could be used as weapons against her. But I couldn't think of anything to stop the spill of words.

"At first, she had good days and bad. She'd play with me, tease me." Kara looked up at me from between damp lashes. "That's what caught me about the 'crabby pants.' That's what she used to call me when I didn't want to behave. I haven't thought of it in years. As time went on, she needed more and more of whatever she was shooting that week to stay high. Instead of going to a supplier, she kept it in her room. The apartment was kept almost freezing to keep it all at top potency."

Dammit. Those small boxes of powder in Sary's storage room. That cold had nearly killed her as a grown woman.

"I left as soon as I could. It was better than slipping out when her 'visitors' came, trying to dodge their hands."

I focused on my breathing, on being there for her. But Ghelfi was a small city. It would be easy enough to find the bastards.

"When I heard that she'd killed herself, I didn't know what to feel. Her landlord gave me a box of her stuff, and I shoved it into a drawer in my apartment. Never even opened it. Don't want to." She sniffled, then straightened her spine. "Not sure what sort of daughter that makes me."

"The kind that does what she can. The kind that survives." I breathed in the smell of her hair. "The kind that kicks ass, usually mine."

She wrapped her arms around my neck and kissed me. "Idiot." Another kiss, longer, slower. "And if we're going to get to Rati before the day is over, we better get going."

Maybe the reflective mood had opened some of her memory. As we passed through the streets she happily pointed out random landmarks and people, recalled odd bits of gossip and rumor. A bunk rack with a flashy holo of faraway green mountains: "They say that the owner of the Highland Arms is an exotic dancer who made her fortune and started a very respectable career closer to the Hub. She keeps the place as a reminder, but makes sure to screw over the guests, just to keep in touch."

A pile of rubble taking up half a block: "That's where enforcers set up a gladiatorial ring years ago. Someone tried to bring in giant Hoorverian rats from the Waste, but they didn't survive long enough for the fights to be popular."

A storefront, solid black, no signage at all, caused her to sigh longingly: "They have the best blades in the entire dome. Pricey, but worth it."

Finally, we stopped in front of a totally nondescript building. She kicked aside the refuse at the front of the door and put her hand on the plate. "Just stand here, where she can get a clear view, alright?"

I moved to where she indicated, looked around. "I don't see any cams." I double checked the corners.

Kara laughed. "You wouldn't. She's very, very good."

The door slid open almost immediately and a small, featureless bot faced us. "I'm so glad you're here!" came a young woman's voice from the speaker. "But..."

"Rati, I know." Kara touched my arm gently. "I vouch for him. His name's Davien."

A long moment, then the bot rolled back without acknowledging me, unblocking the entryway and glowing with a soft light. Kara trailed it, and I followed her, looking around. The dimly lit room was stacked high with junk, but on closer look, the junk all seemed to be in remarkably good shape. The path twisted and turned, other openings leading off deeper into the darkness of the room.

"I'm sorry I didn't intervene when they took you," the bot said suddenly. "I'd told the systems to let me work on my project undisturbed. By the time I pulled out and saw the alarm, you'd already been saved."

Kara patted the bot's top. "It turned out fine. I don't expect you to watch over me all the time, you know?"

I followed the conversation with half an ear. Kara's friend was an AI? Made sense, would be useful. RATI - Remote Access Telemetry Initiative? Technological Infrastructure?

Heck, could be left over from any number of Empire initiatives.

The bot stopped at another door. "I've been reviewing your friend's path since he arrived in the dome. There's some... oddities."

My gut tightened. It could be about going into the Waste without breathing gear. It could be about some of the jobs I'd done for Xavis, working my way up. I mentally reviewed what I could remember of them. Nothing out of the usual, no one permanently maimed. At least, I didn't think so.

Kara put her hands on her hips. "I'm sure there are. And I'm sure he's told me about them."

"You know I don't like new people," the bot sounded sulky. I'd never heard an AI sulk.

"We can go if you want." Kara rolled her eyes.

"I can wait outside," I interjected. "If there's information, we need it." I turned, started to work my way back through the maze.

"Stop." The bot sounded resigned. "Kara says you're alright. And I saw you take care of her after those thugs took her. I may not be good with new people, but you're alright. Probably."

"Um... how much did you see?" I refused to be embarrassed about what an AI saw. But Kara seemed just as interested in the question.

"Come on down," the voice laughed, and the bot stood aside to reveal a lift tube.

Once we stopped, Kara led the way past more bots scurrying on unknown tasks, muttering about privacy. We stood under a light mist that smelled of antiseptics, and I tensed. An AI with components that could be infected? The only other technologi-cal/living hybrid I'd seen lately was the Helmet Heads.

Kara looked at me as we stepped out. "What's wrong? She doesn't mean to be rude, just doesn't get a lot of visitors."

Fighting our way past the bots, finding our way to street level, back through the maze. I could do it. We could do it. Plans, options, rolled through my mind. I slowed my breathing further, ready to drop into the dance of combat.

In the middle of a room lit by screens, I could see the back of a metal-encased hoverchair, slowly rotating towards us.

"What'cha working on now?" Kara bounced up to it, and my heart went into my throat. That wasn't in the plan.

"Same quasar computing project." Human hands pushed up, released the enclosure, and it slid away, revealing a very human woman of about Kara's age, long braid pulled over one shoulder, encased in a hover chair. Unlike Xavis, who, as far as I could tell, used his out of a combination of laziness and power trip, it looked like she actually needed the mechanical assistance.

The two chattered, not paying me any attention. Good. That was almost very, very embarrassing. Not an AI. Not a hybrid. What was she?

The dark-haired woman rolled forward. "Hello, I'm Rati Bergere. Kara says I'm happy to meet you."

Kara didn't say anything, but stuck her tongue out at her friend.

"I've got some programs running. Let's get some tea." Rati eyed me cautiously. "I don't know if I have furniture that will hold you."

"Not a problem. I'm pretty used to it."

She turned and led the way past the screens and into an open, airy room. After the clutter of the rest of the space, the pale walls and minimal furniture felt like taking a long, clearing breath.

Kara settled into a low-slung, overstuffed chair, and I sat on the floor near her, hands in plain sight. Rati clearly wasn't comfortable around me, no matter if Kara vouched for my presence. I could at least try to seem non-threatening.

"Oh, hey, Bani and Hoyt are moving the littles over to the old refinery control center," Kara said as she took a cup of steaming tea from Rati.

"Do they need help? I could send a bot or two, move some of the rubble, check the structure over." Rati chewed on a nail, eyes focused somewhere else. "Maybe I can custom fit something that would be easier for them to control, rather than relying on me remoting."

"That'd be great. They can use all the help they can get."

Rati paused before filling the second cup. "Would you like some?"

"Only if it's convenient." A glance at the small table showed that she'd only expected one guest.

"Easy enough." Her fingers flew over the armrest of the chair, and another bot rolled into the room, a third, identical cup in its padded pincers.

"Thank you," she said absently as she took it. "Now," she poured the third cup of steaming tea and sat back in her chair, eyes flicking over both of us. "What are you looking for?"

"We need to find Helmet Head," Kara popped up.

For the first time since we entered her lab, Rati looked startled. "Who?"

"You know, that weirdo that took my dust."

"Of course." Rati tapped her fingers against the side of the cup. "Is he not at the coordinates?"

"Not when we were last there. He's got to have someplace else he's using for a base, some other hiding place." Kara scowled. "Bastard took my haul, and I need it back."

Rati sighed. "This… might be complicated."

Kara sloshed her tea, but didn't notice. "What?"

"The city's camera system has been hijacked." Rati cracked a grin. "By someone other than me, I mean. And I haven't been able to get back in for hours. I've been in the ice, trying to crack it, but whoever took it over is good."

Doubt wove through Kara's voice. "Better than you?"

Rati thought, sipped her tea. "Maybe not better, but fast. Almost inhumanly so. I'd think it was an AI if I didn't know all the ones in this sector. And the ones I know would have said something if a new one came in."

Kara looked at me, and I shrugged. "Maybe. I'm as lost about their tech as anyone."

"Who else could it be," she snapped back. "Maybe it had the sense to do what we planned - use the city cameras to find us before we found it?"

Rati's eyes followed us. "It'll be easier to help if I have all the info, you know."

"The Helmet Head," I ran my hand through my hair, stalling. "This is going to sound nuts if you didn't see it, but it's some weird hybrid human/android. Could it be the one blocking you? Directly interfacing with the systems?"

"Possibly." Her gaze speared Kara. "So, it was a new kind of android, and you didn't bring me one? After I asked, and everything?"

I thought about the mess of writhing flesh, wrapped around the dull gray metal, cracked dome spilling open. "I really, really don't think it would be a good idea." A spark of inspiration hit. "But if we find the second one, I'll try to find a way to bring at least a sample of it back to you."

Rati's fingers tapped the side of her cup again, thinking. "We just need to find a way to locate him, then, and without the cameras. Maybe start running a trace on the servers he's using to block me?"

Kara interrupted. "I've been thinking. Do we really need to find it?"

My neck almost sprained, turning to look at her so quickly. "What? That was the plan. Find him, find the dust, get off-planet. That was the plan, right?"

"I know," she murmured, eyes almost closed, thinking, "but I think we've got it the wrong way 'round."

I waited, almost able to watch the wheels spin in her head.

"We need the dust for two things, right? Get the credits for a ship, and to finish the deal with Xavis."

I nodded.

"But dust has no history, no way to say who's the owner of which particular pile," she continued. "That's why I went after it, to begin with."

"True..." I was trying to catch up, really I was. But I couldn't see how that made a difference right now.

Her face lit up like a kid opening a present, with sheer glee. "We don't need that dust, any will do."

Aha. Like a kid opening up a present of chaos and house-breaking.

"We do another hit on Sary's. There was plenty more in that safe, I just didn't get a chance to remove it."

I stared at her. "Are you forgetting that's how you got into all of this? And it seems likely he's moved the contents of the safe since you burned a hole in it?

"Nope, haven't forgotten a thing. But unless you have a better idea, I think we should go with it."

I thought. It was true, we didn't technically need to find the Helmet Head. I wanted to know what was on its commtower, but the intercept should have sent that to my datapad back in my quarters by now.

I wanted to know where their base was, who was behind the Hunters... but I had a feeling even if we found it, there wasn't a way to get that information from it. Although, I'd have liked a chance to take that Hunter on again. But that wasn't particularly helpful.

"You're saying it's time to change the plan."

"Nope," she shook her head vigorously. "New plan is the same as the old plan - at least the important parts. Get off Neurea and move from there, right?" She leaned back in the chair, eyes half-closed, tea long forgotten. "We just need to rethink our strategy. Which is easier, faster? Stealing the dust I already stole, or go back and get more?"

"You're forgetting the flaw with both of those options," Rati said.

"Hmm?"

Rati's voice was clipped, impatient. "You don't know where to locate either source. You could waste all the time just finding either our strange visitor or Sary's new depot."

"Couldn't you build a device, a sensor of some sort to locate antonium?" Kara asked. "Remember, you thought the Helmet Head we saw on the tape had something like that. How else could he have found my hiding spot?"

"Of course I could. If I had a few days. Which we don't."

"But what if we knew where a third stash was," I wondered, mostly thinking aloud.

Both women pivoted to me, eyes bright as lasers.

"I have an idea, maybe. But it's walking the fine line between stupid and brilliant." Stupid. Definitely leaning towards stupid.

"Let us decide that," Rati said.

"Why can't it be both?" Kara answered at the same time.

I sipped my tea, sorting my rough thoughts into some kind of order.

"The Tithe..." I started, and Kara choked on her tea, spluttering.

"That's brilliant." She leaned over the edge of the chair to kiss me. "See," she turned, beaming to Rati. "I told you he was wonderful."

"Apparently," Rati said drily, "since the two of you appear to be able to read each other's thoughts. But I'm not entirely sure what you've just decided on. Besides," she grinned at Kara, "if you're that excited about it, I'm still going to weigh in on the side of stupid idea."

"Humph," was Kara's only reply.

"Like I said, it could be either." But Kara's faith in the idea added to my confidence. "Every Tithing Day, people from all over the city bring goods to Xavis. And Kara wasn't the only one planning to pay in dust. It's been too soon for him to have shipped it off-planet, so it's got to be somewhere stored in his complex. And dust knows no provenance."

"We're going to steal his own dust for the tithe," Kara bounced in her chair, a wicked grin on her face. "Best idea ever."

"You know I can't help you once you're in the complex." Rati chewed on her bottom lip, looking worried. "The complex is on a different system than the rest of the city, never found a way in."

"What if we brought you in with us?" I offered.

Now they both looked horrified. "She can't leave," Kara started. "I don't go out," Rati said with an air of finality.

"Who said you had to go in person? From what I can tell, you spend a lot of time remoting, right?"

Rati nodded slowly.

"What if we brought in a program, enough to make a hole from the inside, get you inside Xavis' systems?"

Her eyes lit up. "The security in founder's complex is intricate, but working on it from two directions... Yes, it should be doable."

"And once you're in, you could find where Xavis stores all the good stuff," Kara was nearly rubbing her hands together in anticipation. Once we were off-planet, out of this place, I could tell we'd have to find another outlet for her more unconventional hobbies.

"And once I'm in, he'll never be able to get me out." Rati's eyes were already distant, focused on lines of code no one but her could see. "Once this is inside, it will start worming its way through, like a regular comm. But the signal will have a map encoded, a hole in the security I can get back through."

She took a deep sigh, focus snapping back to the real world. "This is going to take a while, guys."

"How long," Kara said. Our deadline with Xavis approached, and while I could fight off the rest of the enforcers, I'd rather not. At least not without a few more days of healing.

"A couple of hours, at least. I'm sorry."

Kara laughed at Rati's glum expression. "That's no time to wait at all."

She shot me a look full of promise. "I'm sure we can think of plenty of things to do."

KARA

"You want to do what?"

Davien didn't seem as excited as I'd expected.

"Weapons shopping," I repeated. "Supplies. Stuff we'll need for the job, right?" If he didn't have such a strong jawline, I'd have said he was pouting. "What did you think I had in mind?"

He glanced over at the back of Rati's chair. She'd already jacked back in, blind to the world around her.

"I'd been considering some indoor activities."

"Really."

He knelt between my legs, still as tall as I was seated, and pulled me to him, fingers twined in my hair, cradling the back of my head with insistent pressure. "Really."

The demanding kiss left no question of what he wanted, and I immediately opened to the flick of his tongue. My arms twined around his neck and my legs wrapped his waist as if driven by their own desires.

He stood with me still clinging to him, lifting me out of the chair as if I weighed nothing, his arm pulling my hips tighter into him.

"Excuse me."

Gasping, we broke away from each other to stare open-mouthed at Rati.

She rolled her eyes at us, grinning. "I need to move to the lab. You're in the way."

Face burning, I wiggled out of Davien's arms, only a little wobbly on my feet. "Sorry about that, didn't think you'd be noticing things for a while."

Rati rolled on past, shaking her head. "I'm not easily shocked. But you'll be more comfortable in one of the rooms in the back, I'd think." She shot me a look over her shoulder. "I promise to turn the security cams off."

Davien looked as uncomfortable as I felt.

"Actually," I said, slipping my hand into his. "We're going shopping. Anything you need while we're out?"

Rati pulled the immersive virtual screen over her head and shoulders. "No thanks," came her voice from the speakers around us. "I'll tell the bots to let you in if I'm not done by the time you get back."

On the street, Davien looked a little more comfortable. "What do you think we need? We're not going in for a full-on attack, you know."

"I need to replace my knife, at least." I'd been itchy for it for the last three days. Surely we had time to find a replacement. I looked up at him. "Don't you want anything?"

"Blades are fine, but I'm usually ok without. But I'll get you whatever you want." His stomach rumbled as if arguing with him.

"I see. Maybe we should go by Artin's?"

He actually blushed. "Apparently healing up without the medtanks or nutribars takes a lot more food."

"And Artin's curry *is* amazing," I added.

He didn't argue.

This time I only had the one bowl, while Davien polished off three.

"You can have both of the sweets," he promised.

"I don't understand you. They're so good!"

"Then I wouldn't want to deprive you," he replied, stretching back in his chair, no longer devouring everything Artin set in front of him like, well, like a wolf.

By the time Artin brought over the orange confections, business had died down enough for us to talk with him.

"Artin, have you seen Bani?"

Davien scowled at the name, but I ignored him.

"He came by yesterday to help me but said he had another job today. Why?" Artin's brow furrowed. "Is there anything wrong?"

The last thing I wanted to do was add to the old man's worries. "Nope!" I answered as cheerily as I could. "Just keep missing him around town."

I thought for a long moment. If things didn't go well tonight, I wouldn't be back. If things did go well... how much time would I have before Davien wanted to leave?

I hugged Artin, probably startling the hell out of him. I guess I wasn't known to be particularly affectionate, even with the few people I liked.

"Thanks," I muttered.

"I'm more worried now," he replied, then turned a piercing stare on Davien. "I don't know what's going on. I probably don't want to know." He waved one finger close to Davien. "But I know I want her back and safe. Do you understand, young man? Just because I'm old, doesn't mean I'm helpless."

I held my breath, pretty sure Davien wasn't exactly used to being threatened by elderly cooks.

"I promise," was all Davien said, then held his own hand out, but for a handshake. "She'll be safer with me than she's ever been."

Artin snorted but took the offered hand. "That's not saying much, you know."

"Guys, I'm right here?" I said, torn between being annoyed and touched. "I don't usually opt for safe?"

"We know," Davien answered, smirking.

I gave up on them. "Fine. Can we go shopping now?"

"Promised her a new knife," he told Artin.

"Smart man."

I think I liked it better when they weren't talking.

I TOOK Davien to the weapons store we'd passed on the way to Rati's. He'd promised me a knife, I wasn't going to skimp.

"Look at all the pretties," I breathed.

"From what I'd seen, most women prefer jewelry," he answered.

"Then most women are idiots," I answered, only half paying attention. In the display case across the back wall was the most beautiful blade. The perfect length, light gray ceramisteel and wooden hilt, dark stripes through a golden sheen.

"Good eye," the woman behind the counter said. "Untun wood, nearly as hard as ceramisteel itself."

"I need to hold it," I murmured, ignoring Davien's laugh.

"Of course," she answered, and brought it over to me.

It fit like a dream in my hand, the balance as if it were made for me.

I turned to Davien. "This one," I demanded.

He frowned slightly. "Don't you even want to see any others?"

I stroked the back of the blade again, down to the satin finish of the wood. "Trust me. You may not have a use for weapons, but I do. I know what I need."

"Then it's settled." He pulled out a credit spike, but the woman only stared over our shoulders, expression distracted. I turned to see what had caught her attention and heard it. The low rumble of a crowd, growing louder.

She took the knife back from me, locked it away in the case. "I'm sorry, we're closing now."

"But, my knife!" I cried indignantly as she shooed us to the front of the shop.

"Please come back for it tomorrow," she answered as she pulled the grate down behind us, then sealed the doorway with a zip.

I sighed. Every so often it happened. A riot broke out, the pressure of life in the dome erupting in the street, sparked off by the smallest of things and then running havoc until the crowd burned itself out.

Anyone with any sense hunkered down, kept inside and away from it all until the streets were quiet.

But I still wanted my knife.

Davien stared down the street, frowning. "Where do you think they're heading?"

I listened, but the way the sound echoed off the buildings, I couldn't get a fix on it. "No idea. Let's go look."

"Are you serious? We've got a job to do tonight. I don't think getting injured in a riot is going to help our cause any."

"As serious as I ever am." It probably didn't help my case when I stuck my tongue out at him.

I didn't mean look from street level. "Up top is safer."

We headed towards the best perch I could think of close by.

At the top, I could see the armbands of Bedrock Core.

"Damn it. I wish they'd stay out of it."

Davien looked at me, appraisingly. "I thought you didn't like how things are run here?"

"I don't. But this is just going to get a lot of innocent people in trouble. Xavis will have informants in the crowd, watching, taking names. Even if people weren't involved before, they'll find life a lot harder now."

"What do you think should be done?"

I shook my head. I'd wondered and wondered how to break the system. "I don't know. I'd like to just put Xavis, Sary, and all the rest of them in a room and let them fight it out."

"And then?"

"Seal up the door," I cracked. "But solving the city's problem isn't our responsibility today. Just saving our own asses."

I slid down the wall, leaned against it and tried to ignore the sound of the crowd, all the fun of our outing long gone.

"Let's go back and see if Rati's done."

"Even if she's not, a nap wouldn't be a bad thing," Davien answered.

I shot him a look. "Depends on what sort of nap you have in mind."

Rati was finished when we got back. On a tray in the sitting room were two small devices - a standard looking data chip, and a curved, narrow piece of a thin, flexible substance.

"Try that on, Kara, it should stick behind your ear."

I pressed it against my skin, and it clung, tiny suckers holding fast.

"Now you can hear me anywhere," came a whisper, almost in my head.

"That's kinda creepy." I started to pull it off, then thought better of it. What if it didn't stick again?

"Maybe, but useful. Sound comes through your mastoid bone. And you'll barely need to whisper for me to hear you."

Davien nodded his approval, then picked up the other chip. "What sort of port do you need this put into?"

Rati shrugged. "Pretty much anything with general network access will do. It's loaded with every bit of stealth code I know. As soon as the tunnel is made, I'll be able to contact you on the earpiece."

"Is there anything else we need?" I asked.

"A whole lot of luck - but you've always made your own," she smiled.

My heart rode in my throat when we entered the lift tube. I had always hated it here in the complex. The oldest building on Neurea, the founders had dug down, safe from the Waste, while their bots built the city and the dome.

The whole complex had an alien feel - unlike the buildings above ground that had been modified, lived in, and usually run down, the founders' complex had been left alone until the first of the crime lords took it as his fortress. Since then, every successor in the deadly rise to the top had claimed the complex as their own.

It was kept scrupulously clean, but in my mind's eye, the walls ran with blood.

I checked the chrono. "Ten hours left."

Damn it. We needed to find a place for Rati's chip as soon as possible, but for the life of me, I couldn't figure where. Davien's quarters were a no-go. If anyone suspected interference, I didn't want the trail to immediately run back to us.

There had to be something, a place everyone had access to... Eyes focused on nothing, I mentally ran through the public areas of the complex, then startled. One panel on the wall of the lift tube had a slightly different sheen to the metal. Maybe...

I caught Davien's eye, then looked at the panel, hoping he'd catch the idea without saying anything to alert the unquestionably present hidden camera.

At Rati's, I hadn't thought about the difficulties of working with someone else. Maybe I had been on my own for too long. But he moved as if in my own mind, nodding fractionally towards the pocket I'd secreted the chip into before he grabbed me, pushed me against the suspicious panel.

"At least if everything else goes bad," he growled, one hand slipping under my shirt, while the other braced at the panel near my head, shielded from any camera by our bodies, speaking for the microphones, "I'll have the memory of you pinned under me, screaming my name."

His mouth plundered mine, and in the reactor blast of his

passion, I lost track of where we were, what we were doing. A nip at my lower lip between his teeth, and I opened my eyes to see him wink. He'd found it.

I wrapped tighter around him, running my hand over his arm, twining my fingers with his own and slipping him the chip in the process. My attention divided, I could feel the panel move against my back, and flattened my back just a bit more to try to help hold it in place.

Just a moment, and then he tugged the panel gently from me, and the softest of snaps caught my ear as it clicked back into place.

Both hands ran over my sides now, as if nothing had happened, and he breathed into my ear. "Emergency comm station in case of lift tube malfunction. Good eye."

We broke apart as the chime signaled the arrival at our floor.

It was strange coming back to Davien's room. I'd only been here once, just three days ago. I'd hated what I thought he was.

Now, I didn't know what to think.

Stop it, Kara, I chided myself. Daydreaming before a job will get you killed.

He went over to the jump bag and pulled out his datapad.

"Anything interesting? I asked, perching on the bed.

"Figured while we wait, I should see if we have anything from that intercept I planted on the Hunter's commtower. Maybe there's information I can pull about the location of that base, who's running it."

"Or even who the hell they're trading weapons with here," I added.

Davien's eyebrow lifted. "I thought that would be obvious. Sary has my vote. He's looking for ways to get ahead of Xavis, surely he's in the market for new weapons, something no one else has."

I shook my head. "I don't think he'd be able to get past the communications block on the dome. How would he even know where to look for people, robots, whatever, like that?"

"They could both be the buyers," he said with a smirk, "and end up taking care of each other."

I laughed, with only a tinge of the black despair I felt most of the time thinking about the screwed up politics of my home dome. "We'd never be so lucky."

I rolled over on the bed, propped up on my elbows to watch him. "So, what did you get? Answers?"

"Yes and no," he said, scowling.

"It doesn't seem like a gray sort of question."

"I have data, plenty of transmissions -- but it's still decoding. I didn't think it would take so much time to decode."

I shrugged. "Bring it back with us to Rati, when we're done. She handles that sort of stuff to wake up instead of coffee."

"You're pretty sure this is going to work out," he said, slipping the datapad back into the bag.

"I don't have any choice. *We* don't have any choice. Never do, at this stage of the game. If we start doubting when we're already committed, we'll screw up. Happens every time.

"Does it work out, every time?" he asked softly.

"Nope. I'd rather not think about the times a job went bad. But worrying about it, when the dice are rolled, and we're in the thick of it, can't help."

"Did you ever think we could just get out, the hell with finding the dust or anything else and just get off-planet?" Davien's eyes searched my own.

"Xavis meant what he said. He'd send every other enforcer he had to bring us in. The reward would be so high half the dome would be on the streets to find us. Unless you have a ship already waiting, we'd never get out."

Davien shook his head, lips pressed into a thin line.

"Then we stick to the plan."

"What is this now, plan C, or D? Maybe the plan needs some

additions," he leaned over me on the bed, eyes alight with promises.

"Oh no," I pushed him away. "Any minute now, Rati's going to break through, and we need to be ready."

"We're ready now," he shrugged.

"Do you really want her listening in?" I tapped the earpiece for emphasis.

He sat back on his heels. "Right. I've got a deck of cards around here somewhere."

It only took four hands of Tonk before I heard a buzz.

"I'm in," Rati's voice was the merest whisper. "Running searches through maps now."

I stood up, tossing my hand down on the bed. "Lousy cards anyway. Time to get ready."

Davien tidied the deck and slipped them into the jump bag. "I'm ready to get out of here."

"Not planning on coming back?" I nodded at the bag, now thrown over his shoulder.

"I'll be happy to never see this place again."

"No good memories at all?" I let my eyes rest on the patch of floor that he'd pinned me to three days ago when this mad adventure first started.

He grinned. "Maybe that." He wrapped his arms around me and nuzzled my neck. "But if I had to pick between here and the Imperial, let's get back to the bunk rack."

A soft cough. "I have the maps ready, if you two aren't going to be otherwise occupied."

I broke away from Davien, face flushed.

"Three levels up from where you are, then go left from the stairs."

We followed Rati's instructions through the maze of corridors until we stood in front of a locked door.

"Now what," I whispered.

"You don't have to be so loud," she complained. "Give me a minute."

It slid open, and she giggled. "Used Xavis' print in the register. Let them figure that out, when they go through the access logs."

A wide room, filled with shelves, but instead of the neatly organized inventory I'd imagined, jumbled piles of items spilled from one rack to the next.

"From the records, it looks like he only allows access to this room to one person at a time. And," her voice choked a little, "it doesn't look like a job with long-term survivorship."

"Well," I said, looking at the mess, "that's a great way to mess up your record keeping. Does he even know what's in here?"

"Maybe," she answered. "But probably not exactly. And, to be honest, I'm not sure if I'm going to be able to tell you where to start searching."

I checked my chrono again. "That's fine, between the two of us, we'll pull it off."

We started near the front, with the thought that the most recent tithes would be closer to the door, with less crap piled on them.

"Anything?" I called over to Davien.

"Nothing yet, lots of things that would be interesting another day, but no dust."

"Damn it," I muttered. This was supposed to be the easy job.

"Seriously, Rati, in your spare cycles, a sensor wouldn't be a bad thing."

"I'll add it to the list, I promise," came the ghostly voice in my ear.

A long, tense few minutes passed before my hand closed on a familiar shape.

"Got one!"

I glanced again at the chrono - at this rate, I didn't know if we were going to find enough in time.

"Two more over here," Davien called.

"Come on, Kara," I muttered to myself. "Let's go for a big haul."

The glint of a vial caught my eye. "There we go…. Damn it. Just one.

"If they got handed in at every Tithe, he wouldn't have been so anxious to make that deal", Davien reminded me.

"Yeah, but it shouldn't be that hard to find. As valuable as they are, you'd think he would keep better track of them."

"Probably he's already sold or traded the ones that could be found easily. Besides," he said, and I could hear his smirk even with two shelving units between us, "I thought you liked a challenge."

"You're enough of a challenge for me," I teased back.

I started rummaging through a stack of soft fabric, hoping to find something tucked into its folds.

"Kara," Rati whispered after a few more minutes of our searching, "there's someone else by the door. I can't make out who it is."

"Hide," I whispered to Davien.

Davien moved silently beside me, between me and the unknown, and we'd barely slipped behind a densely packed rack when the door opened, and a hooded figure walked in.

I bit back a gasp and squeezed Davien's hand. Hard to tell who was under the hood and scarf, but it was the same optical pattern as the guy Hoyt had met with earlier.

He made no pretense at stealth, just moved to the closest rack and started tossing items aside, as if frantically searching for something. He was so intent on the piles of goods that he didn't notice Davien step behind him and drop a club-like fist on the back of his head.

"What did you do that for," I gasped, looking at the figure sprawled on the ground.

"He's not dead," Davien sounded offended. "And we're on the clock, right?"

"Well, it makes it easier to see who he is, at least. It bugs me.

He's familiar, but that stupid pattern…" I pulled back the hood and lowered the scarf.

"Oh Void," I rocked back on my heels. "It's Juda."

"Who?" Davien sounded as puzzled as I felt.

"My ex…." Shaky legs straightened up, kept me moving away from his limp form as if on autopilot. "The one who took my savings before the tithe, and disappeared. I didn't know he was part of Bedrock Core. But what's he doing here?"

Davien frowned. "And how did he get in? I'll assume your friend wasn't helping?"

I shook my head, still stunned that Juda was here. "Rati hated him. And he didn't have the skills to break in on his own."

"Then he's got friends of his own."

After a long moment of thought, he grabbed a strip of the fabric and swiftly bound Juda's hands and feet. "I don't like surprises, and we don't have time to figure this out."

He straightened up, dusted his hands on his pants. "Plan modification. We have enough for the first stage."

"What?" Not a brilliant reply, but I couldn't keep up, knocked off balance still by Juda's presence, unconscious as it was.

Davien was unfazed. "Like you said, take it back to basics. We don't need to get Xavis eight vials tonight - just the four."

"But then, how are we getting off Neurea?" I countered. "We're relying on that extra dust to buy passage on a ship."

Davien waved at the storage racks. "Keep searching. There's gotta be more than just dust in here we can use for that." He slung the jump bag off his shoulder and handed it to me.

I took it, thinking. He was right. I'd gotten so caught up in the plan, I'd forgotten there was always another way.

"Do you think Rati can get us back in here?"

Davien shook his head. "No need. I'll meet with Xavis, you stay here and search."

Relief washed over me. Being in the complex was bad enough,

facing Xavis again wasn't on my top ten list of things to do. Hell, not on my top million list.

"Are you sure?" I knew it was ridiculous to worry about Davien, but I couldn't seem to help it. "I'm not comfortable with us splitting up."

"Positive. His deal is with me, not you." Davien's voice sounded oddly flat. "Makes more sense for you to stay here, find what we can use."

"I'll be able to keep an eye on your beau for you, most of the way," Rati whispered. "Haven't broken into the hall's cameras yet, but I can watch everything else."

My cheeks flamed. Davien wasn't my beau, not exactly. I had no idea what he was, what we were. And now wasn't the time to think about it.

Davien moved towards the door without waiting for me. "Have your friend let you know when I'm done, and we'll get out of here."

I followed him, confused. Something was off, but I couldn't get him to face me. "And what should I do about *him*?"

He paused in front of the door, back rigid. "Up to you." The door slid open, and he walked away.

"He's just thinking about the job," Rati whispered. "You should be, too."

I nodded, shoving back an unexpected pang. Seriously, I was going to be upset about being separated from him for half an hour? I'd never been a clingy woman, and I wasn't going to start now.

I wasn't a good woman, either. I semi-gently nudged Juda's body out of my way and stared at the shelf. He'd walked straight to that rack, no looking around, and no hesitation. Whatever he wanted, it was here. And if he wanted it, it was likely valuable.

Boxes flew as I searched, more thoroughly than he'd bothered to, trying not to think about Davien facing Xavis, or his strange behavior when he'd left. Rati was right, he just had his head in the game.

There, something felt odd. A small cloth bag, nothing special, but a touch heavier than I expected. I ran it through my hands again. Near the bottom seam, something flat and hard stiffened the fabric.

I found a cheap knife on a nearby shelf and slit it open. A comm chip, no markings, paired with a credit chip. Not enough to get us off-planet. Not nearly enough. My fist clenched around the chips. There had to be more.

A cough sounded from near my feet. "Kara? What are you doing here?"

Juda blinked, messy blond hair now free from the hood, falling half over his eyes in a way I'd thought cute, once upon a time. Now he just looked like a half-grown boy-man.

"I could ask the same of you." I snapped. "And since I'm not the one tied up on the floor, I think I will."

For the first time since I'd met him, he looked something like ashamed. "I fucked up. There was something that got mixed in my tithe that shouldn't have been there."

"You mean, my credits?" Even if it ended up with Davien and me being a pair, the fury over Juda's betrayal lingered.

"Well, yeah. Figured you'd make it back." He shrugged, and I could have choked him for his nonchalance. "You always do. No, this was serious."

"You wouldn't know serious if it hit you."

Juda's eye's narrowed. "Yeah, well, I'm not the one going around with one of Xavis' hit men."

That time I 'nudged' him a little harder, just once. Or twice.

"Start again, but don't get personal. You really don't want to do that."

"Fine. Look, you've got to help me."

"No, I don't. You're a jerk who stole from me. And I can't believe you're working for Bedrock."

"Just little jobs, mostly running messages, making a few credits where I can. Old sneakernet stuff, right? Avoid the comms monitors. And that's where I fucked up."

He took a long breath. "I had a chip I was bringing from one bigshot to another. But the guy taking the tithe took the bag with the credit spike in it when he logged me through. I couldn't figure out how to get it back without causing a scene."

Juda looked down, mumbling. "They don't think Xavis has read it, but if it gets fed into a system, it'll compromise all kinds of stuff."

I eyed him disbelievingly. I'd actually thought this idiot was attractive? "What 'kind of stuff?'" I asked, not bothering to hide the sarcasm that fairly dripped from my voice.

"I don't know." He looked frantic. "You gotta believe me, Kara, they don't tell me much."

A short bark of laughter escaped me. "I believe that perfectly well."

I thought about the chip I'd found, held the bag up in front of him. "Any chance this is it?"

He squirmed in his bonds. "Yes, you've got it! Give it to me!"

"Shut up, Juda". I turned away from him. I needed to think.

"But..."

"Shut up, or I'll walk out of here with the bag," I promised.

He was quiet. Maybe he finally realized he'd pushed me too far.

Whatever I thought about Bedrock, I didn't want them betrayed to Xavis. Other people shouldn't pay for Juda's stupidity.

However, I didn't want him complicating my life any further. And I still had a room to search for something, anything, valuable.

I slipped the two chips into my jacket, then turned back to him.

"Here's the deal. I have my own job going on. I don't need you in my way." I placed the bag twenty feet from him, the knife on top. "You can cut yourself free, take it, and get out." I stood up, walked back into the further reaches of the room. "But shut up about it, or I'll gag you, as well."

It wouldn't take me ten minutes to reach that knife. Juda would be out of my hair for another hour. Muffled grunts were all I heard for the next few minutes until another whisper in my ear.

"Kara, we have a problem."

"What?"

"I found that Hunter."

"Great, but unless you find the bag as well, he's not much good to us."

"Kara, he's here." Fingers of ice sliced my belly.

"Where?"

"The hall. I just broke into the cameras. Davien just walked in." Rati sounded frantic. "Kara, the Hunter is there."

DAVIEN

The stairwells were quiet as I descended to Xavis' reception hall on the deepest level.

Hoyt and Bani must have already moved the littles. It was for the best that they'd gone, safer to be anywhere but here, and they deserved a better place to play, but I missed catching my little flying girl.

Maybe I'd stop by and check on Mavi when this was over, before we left. I stopped frozen, mid-step. What was I thinking?

More importantly, what was I doing, getting this attached to Kara?

Kara's startled announcement that the creep on the floor was her ex had thrown me. Was that the sort of person she should be with? Maybe not that one, he was obviously a loser. But, shouldn't she be with someone who was at least human?

I ran my tongue over the tips of my teeth and tasted blood. And someone not as likely to drag her into the middle of a war?

She hadn't listened before. Once we were free of Xavis' threat, I'd make her understand. It was for the best, even if it killed me inside.

I clenched the vials of dust. Such small, fragile things to

weigh against the balance of our lives. Kara might not find any more upstairs, but I was sure that, with her thief's instincts, she'd find enough of something else valuable to get us off-planet.

Or, at least, her and Bani. Once the bargain was over, there was no reason I couldn't just keep working for Xavis as an enforcer. That had been my plan from the beginning, to work and save up to buy passage. It would be a good, uncomplicated plan to go back to.

For the first time since I'd started working for Xavis, only silence greeted me when I stepped into the small room leading to the reception hall.

Maybe Xavis had gone on one of his tirades, and everyone was hiding. Not uncommon. Anyone who could get out of his sight did, when he was in that mood.

I shook my head. That sort of lack of impulse control must be a recent development. I couldn't imagine how he'd made it to the top of the scheming pile of criminals infesting Ghelfi City with that temper. Maybe it was at the same time he'd decided to use the hoverchair - an odd combination of laziness and intimidation technique.

I pushed open the doors to the hall and took stock. It was quiet here, too.

Maybe it wasn't just Xavis' lack of focus I should be worrying about. My own failure to pick up strangeness in my environment would get me killed faster.

The monitors around the hall were unmanned. Only Xavis himself remained, upon his dais, inspecting something on a side table beside him. The background of deep scarlet curtains threw his bulk into sharp relief.

"Xavis," I called out. "I've come to settle our deal."

He jerked back in his chair, as if his mind had been elsewhere. "Davien, my boy. I'm happy to see you."

His voice had a brightness I'd never heard before. I stopped halfway across the floor, senses stretched out as far as I could. Something was seriously wrong.

"I'm pleased that you were able to uphold your end of our bargain." He floated towards me in that damn hoverchair. "You're one of my best men, and, despite her occasional inconveniences, Kara is a talent I'd hated to be Wasted." He tittered at his bad joke.

"I have your four vials. So her tithe is paid, and we've met the deadline, right?"

He waved his hand, eyes glittering. "Of course. Everything's back to normal."

Sure, I thought. I still couldn't hear anything out of place, but every nerve screamed that it was time to be somewhere else.

Xavis stopped mere inches from me, hand outstretched.

I placed the vials in his palm and made a quick nod. "Now that this is out of the way, I'll leave you to your evening."

I'd started to the door when he called out. "Wait."

I froze.

"Our deal was for the vials that Kara had stolen, and that she claimed a mysterious helmeted figure had stolen from her in turn, was it not?" His voice oozed with malice.

"Right," I gestured to the vials in his hand. "Half of that eight would be those four."

"But these can't be those vials," he continued, a greasy smile curling his lips.

"How do you figure that?" I fought the urge to stiffen, to brace for a fight. So far, he didn't have anything on us, giving the game away with my reaction would be a fool's move.

"Dust knows no provenance, as I'm sure you've heard. But some things do." He floated back towards his dais and picked up a small satchel from the table next to him

"Like this." He ran his finger over the strap, flipped open the flap to show me the twinkle of eight vials in their pockets. I didn't recognize the bag, but I didn't have to. It had to be Kara's. But how could it be here?

Unless.

"Perhaps you've already been introduced to my guest?"

Xavis beckoned and, out of the shadows of the drapery, a Hunter silently emerged.

Oh shit.

It stopped by Xavis' chair, but I could feel the full force of its attention from beneath the black helmet. "Results of the Daedalus Experiment are to be returned to Base," it finally said.

"Hmmm…" Xavis mused. "That doesn't sound pleasant. And it would leave Kara without her new defender."

My gut clenched, and I readied for the fight.

"It's a deal. He's yours."

KARA

"*Make* it go faster," I muttered, pacing the lift tube like a cage.

"I've already taken all but the safeties off the controls," Rati answered. "Just a few more seconds."

"Can you at least warn Davien, somehow?" I begged her.

Her voice was grim. "He already knows. Xavis nearly ordered that thing to fight him."

My heart clenched. Davien hadn't even had a chance to finish healing from the last fight with that thing. It would kill him.

And I would be powerless to do anything other than watch.

Wouldn't I?

My thoughts spun. If Xavis could order it to fight, he could make it stop. I just had to make it worth his while.

I leaned against the comm panel Davien had pushed me against, felt the scorch of his lips on mine all over again.

Xavis would want me back in the complex, under tighter control.

Would that be enough?

I could increase my tithe - didn't know how, but I'd find a way to manage it.

There was nothing Xavis loved more than money. He didn't need to do anything further to Davien.

Davien could get out of here, surely he had some credits saved. I could make more, get him off-planet.

And I'd stay here. Promise Xavis anything, if he'd just stop the fight.

The lift tube finally freed me to burst into the hall. My stomach rose to my throat, mind dizzied as I tried to keep up with the shapes of Davien and the Hunter as they grappled, rolling through the room.

I knew Davien wasn't human. Really, I did. But it wasn't until I watched him fight the Hunter, both of them moving at super-fast speeds, ducking punches that left holes in the walls and would have killed a normal man, that it really sunk in.

And I didn't care.

I had to save him.

"Xavis," I screamed, running to the dais, forcing my attention away from the fight. "Stop it!"

"Why should I do that, little one?" He floated towards me, attention still over my shoulder.

"Because you don't get anything out of it? And I can make you a better deal."

"Really?" He flicked his eyes to me. "What would do that?"

"Increase my tithe." I ran the numbers in my head, gave up, and blurted out something that sounded reasonable. "Fifteen percent more for the next twelve payments. It's far more than you'd get just by having him killed."

I could hear the battle raging behind me, but I couldn't look. All that mattered now was keeping Xavis' attention on me.

"Fifteen percent," I repeated. "You know I can do it."

"Twenty," he replied, eyes glittering.

"Seventeen," I countered.

"Seventeen, for twenty payments." His hungry expression sickened me, but there was no choice.

"Done," I said before he retracted the offer.

He handed me his hand, and I shook it, my belly turning to lead.

I'd never be free. Honestly, I wasn't sure I'd be able to pull off that much of an increase in the tithe. But Davien would escape, and take Bani with him. It would be worth it.

"My friend," Xavis called out. Obviously, the Hunter either didn't hear him or didn't care, because the fight continued, the figures slower now, but unyielding.

The Hunter and Davien's arms locked around each other in a grotesque parody of an embrace. With a sudden twist, the Hunter gained the advantage and flung Davien against the far wall.

He hit with a sickening thud, and my heart caught in my throat. He didn't stand. He didn't move. I couldn't see if he was even breathing.

I pulled against Xavis' grip, but he refused to relent.

"My friend, a word." The mildness of his words underscored the violence soaking through the room.

The Hunter stopped mid-step, then turned slightly towards Xavis.

Davien didn't move. I couldn't pay attention to anything but his battered form.

"I'll see that he's secured." Xavis tapped the control panel of the hover chair, and three of his soldiers entered the room, standing over Davien's body.

"But I'll double the payment for the weapons, if I could ask you to do me a favor. Just to make a little point." His hand squeezed mine painfully, bending it back against the wrist.

"You need to understand you can't bargain with me. I own you, and everyone in Ghelfi City."

"I'm sending you a set of coordinates." He tapped again, and I blinked away tears, either from the pain or watching Davien's chest slowly rise and fall, I wasn't sure.

Wake up, wake up, I breathed.

ELIN WYN

"Destroy the building there, and I'll double the payment for the weapons."

No response from the Hunter.

Xavis' mouth tightened in annoyance. "You do want to get the best price, don't you?"

Seconds stretched until the Hunter replied. "If the experiment is not secured, the payment will be tripled."

Xavis nodded. "Agreed." Another twist to my wrist. "You see, Kara, there's no way out. You think I don't know what happens in my own domain?"

Mind reeling, I could only stutter. "Where are you sending it?"

"Filthy little traitors, thought they could leave. No one leaves," Xavis answered.

Leave? Oh, Void. "Not the refinery?" I whispered.

"Why not?" Xavis shrugged as the Hunter walked out of the room, implacable doom in its march.

"I hear you," Rati whispered in my ear. "I've got bots on the way, but I don't know if it'll be enough."

"How can you do this?" I gasped.

"Children are expendable." Xavis shrugged. "I thought you, of all people, knew that."

Bastard.

"You don't own me. You don't own anyone," I hissed. Fuck the pain. With everything I had left, I pulled him towards me in that stupid chair and punched him between those piggy eyes.

"You bitch," he screamed, as he released me to frantically stab at the controls, moving back to the safety of his dais. "Kill her!"

The three soldiers moved to form a half circle, herding me like easy prey.

Turning their back to Davien, who rose behind them like a thing of nightmares. Blood streamed down his face, split by a mad grin, showing all his pointed teeth.

Before two of the soldiers could turn around, he'd tossed them

176

aside like playthings. He shook the third until my scream caught his attention.

"The Hunter. He's after the children!"

He flung the final soldier against the foot of the dais and turned his wild eyes on me.

"What about you?" The words came out in ragged gasps, but he glared at Xavis, now cowering in his chair.

"I'll be right behind you. I'm safe," I promised. "Don't wait for me."

I leaned into his chest, heart breaking. I didn't know if he'd survive another bout with the Hunter, but neither of us could live with ourselves if we didn't try.

His arms wrapped around me, and he breathed in, nuzzling my hair as if it could give him enough strength. In seconds, he released me and turned away to race through the door.

"Rati, help him," I begged.

I started after him, knowing that at only human speed, I'd never catch him, only be there to witness the aftermath.

Xavis cackled hysterically behind me. "I own you. Never forget it. The only way out is the one your mother took."

I spun, words hot in my throat, then stopped.

In the depths of the scarlet drapery, a flicker caught my eye. A flash of a pattern that didn't want to resolve. Apparently, Bedrock had decided to strike.

I left Xavis to his fate, and ran to follow mine.

DAVIEN

I flung myself onto the street outside the complex. The Hunter was long gone.

But I didn't need to follow him, I knew where he was going.

How to get there before him?

I scanned the area, wishing Kara was with me with her knowledge of the city's alleyways and shortcuts, and...

Roofs.

That would do it.

I scaled the nearest building with a conveniently placed pile of trash, wincing as I went, wishing the damn scalp wound would stop bleeding.

If I didn't get a chance to heal, at least a little, there was no way I could win.

But the thing inside that helmet wouldn't hesitate to destroy the building, kids inside or not.

Heal later, fight now.

With a running start, I leaped from one roof to the next, in fast succession. Each landing jarred my bones just enough to decide this was one of those ideas that fell somewhere between lousy or brilliant, or maybe both.

With a start, I jolted out of my haze. I'd run out of roof. More exactly, the gap between my last roof and the refinery control center was too wide, even for me.

Fine.

I half-slid down the pipes, to stand in front of the building, listening. Nothing from inside, but from the direction of Xavis' complex a commotion of angry shouts and frightened screams was headed my way.

I'd made it here before him, then.

I stuck my head inside and shouted, "Evacuate. Get out!" No response. "Bani! Hoyt! Get the kids and get out!"

With no more time than for that brief warning, the Hunter arrived.

It stopped across the street from me. "All results-"

I cut it off. "Yeah, I've heard it. Not happening."

"You were to be restrained." It seemed to be calculating, thinking.

"I'm sure I was. But that deal wasn't with me."

"You are in my way."

"And I intend to stay here."

It paused for only a moment, while I held my breath. If it really needed to return me to wherever its base was, did that mean it shouldn't kill me? That'd be nice, but it hadn't seemed to be holding back too much in either of our last two fights.

It took a step towards me. "You will be restrained, then I will execute the client's request, and the payment to us will be increased accordingly."

Another step, then a slow, implacable stride that sped up until it charged like a tank.

I braced myself. In the shape I was in, I couldn't put on the speed to avoid it. Nothing to do but hope to use its own speed against it, turn it as it passed, hopefully into something large and solid.

But before it reached me, a wall of junk rose behind me. A bot, so battered I couldn't tell its original purpose, dashed by on its low treads, one steel extension held in front of it like a spear.

The Hunter sidestepped, twisted the metal bar off, and threw it to the side, only to be hit by two smaller bots, both looking as if they'd been rescued from the trash heap.

It wasn't until the tinny speaker on one of them began shouting that I snapped, recognizing the voice through the distortion.

Rati had joined the fight.

A third, larger bot stomped up, and I rolled out of the way, scooping up the discarded bar from the first. This one had a large jaw-like attachment at the front, probably for crushing ore, some detached part of my mind decided.

The Hunter threw the smaller of the bots at me, missing only by fractions of an inch. Shrapnel caught my back as it shattered on the exterior wall of the refinery.

No more time for catching my breath. Even if the bots were slowing it down, they weren't enough to stop it.

I circled around while the Hunter grappled with the large bot, finally wrenching the jaws off it, flinging them away.

This time I ducked, springing back to crack it on the side of the head with my improvised polearm.

I couldn't afford to be caught in the Hunter's grip again. If I could manage it, this would have to be a fight kept at a distance. But that was a pretty big if.

Before I could take another whack at it, another bot crashed into the Hunter's side, grinding its tires into the street, attempting to shove the Hunter back from the control center.

"Get it!" crackled from the speaker, and I thrust and spun in time with the barrage of bots until once again the Hunter freed itself and moved another pace forward.

I tripped back, still out of range, but panting from exertion.

It was halfway across the street now. Between the bots and myself, we'd made it fight for every step.

But how many could Rati send against the monster?

And how long could I stay standing?

And, damn it, how long until the kids got out? I hadn't gotten much of a look at the building when Kara and I had been by, the lift tube had been gutted, so they'd have to take the long way, down the stairs.

But I heard nothing behind me, no movement. Not a sound.

The Hunter took on another bot, and we continued our dance, I struck but felt my blows doing less and less damage. I hadn't even cracked the damn helmet yet.

Another wave of bots and I darted closer. This time I'd knock the dome clear off the bastard's head. This time I'd end this. This time...

I'd be just a little too slow.

The Hunter caught the bar in his hand and used the leverage to throw me over its shoulder. I skidded when I hit the street, pavement burning through the rips of my pants.

Slowly I pushed up on my elbows, then to my knees.

Not done, not done yet. Couldn't let it past.

A low rumble caught my attention. Around the corner came an old roller wagon, pincer arms in the front, clicking and snapping, as it aimed for the Hunter

A wave of bots of any and all description came down the street, piling onto the Hunter as if he were magnetized, not doing much damage, but slowing him down long enough for the cavalry to arrive.

The pincers grabbed the Hunter, and this time the black-clad shape went flying, crashing into the wall of the control center.

A cascade of rubble showered down on it as it struggled to get up. The roller wagon pinned it, but the Hunter pushed back, inch by inch.

"Stay down, you bastard." I pushed the rest of the way to my feet, grabbing up a length of pipe as I staggered towards the wall. This was my chance to finish it.

Until, with a scream of metal, a sheet of permasteel dislodged from the face of the building, plummeting edge first into the black dome.

Shrieking and kicking, the Hunter writhed and was finally still.

I took another step towards it, then closed my eyes to try to make the world stop moving.

But when I looked again, I realized it wasn't my eyes, the building was swaying.

Between the bots, the Hunter, and age, the building had taken all it could, and was on the edge of collapse.

And I still hadn't heard the kids come out.

I limped through the clouds of dust of the ground floor, "Bani, Hoyt!"

Finally, I heard them, scared whimpers, muffled sobs.

"Over here!" I shouted. "Get out!"

Eyes wide, faces smeared with dust, Hoyt and Bani emerged, herding the littles between them.

"Is that all of them?" I pushed them towards the door, too tired to try to soften my words.

Hoyt's shoulders sagged as he shook his head. "The stairway collapsed. Mavi was on the other side."

I froze. "And you left her?"

"I told her to get back to the window," Bani shouted as he tugged me outside. "I can climb up, get her from there."

I searched until I found her tiny shape framed in the window. All the way up. Of course.

The walls shuddered, and another section of permasteel crashed down.

"No way, it's too unstable," I said grimly.

"I'm light," Bani argued. "I can do it."

"Kid, Kara would kill me if anything happened to you. I'm going to count on you to take care of her."

His eyes filled with tears. "But we can't leave Mavi!"

"I'm not planning to." I looked at the window again. I was heavier than Bani, but faster, no matter what the kid thought.

I started figuring my approach. It could work.

Just as I started up, another crash drove me back.

There had to be another way.

"Can you catch me?" a small voice drifted down.

"Mavi," I shouted. "Stay there!"

"What are you going to do?" Hoyt yelled.

"Shut up," I growled, watching Mavi, listening to the creak of the building. The whole damn thing was going to come down. "Get the rest of those kids out of here."

The tension spiraled in my gut as I weighed options. And then, like a kiss of light, a familiar hand was on my shoulder.

"You've got her," Kara whispered from behind me. "She'll be fine." The tension disappeared with her touch, leaving only clear focus.

"Come on down, honey!" I shouted, and damn me if I wasn't rewarded with a giggle.

"Catch me!" Mavi shouted, and she flung herself down.

I shifted, adjusted for her arc, grabbed her from the air and tucked and rolled with her down the street.

We rolled to a stop, and I unfolded from around her. She sighed and leaned her tiny body into my chest.

"We could do that again. But not for a while."

I leaned back, searching the street until I found Kara, grinning like a mad thing.

Our eyes met, and even with rubble and dust all around us, all was right with the world.

KARA

I watched Davien's chest as if each rise and fall was tied to my own heartbeat.

We'd made our way back to Rati's - Davien, me, and all the littles, surrounded by an escort of bots. There was nowhere else safe to go.

Mavi curled up with him, having refused to leave his side except for the brief wash in the decontaminant chamber.

Hoyt and Rati worked the comms, muttering quietly while the rest of the littles sprawled out on hastily built pallets. Bani had finally lost the battle to stay awake, face smoothed in sleep, maybe cleaner than I'd ever seen him.

Hoyt dropped beside me. "Sary and his lieutenants are fighting among themselves for control of the city. No one's noticed that Rati's still inside the systems at the complex."

I shrugged, too exhausted to feel much of anything. "I tried to tell you. Nothing will change." I remembered a flicker of camo. "Did you know about the hit on Xavis?"

His jaw tightened and, in that moment, he looked older than any teenager should. "It was no more than he'd ordered for any number of people." He reached over to flick a blanket back over a child. "Right now, there's chaos, but it'll work out for the best."

"What do you mean?"

"Whoever wins, they won't have real control for months. We can take them down, even if we have to do it one by one."

I shut my eyes, leaning against the wall. The tiniest hope flickered in my gut.

"Take back the city." I breathed, almost afraid to say it aloud. "Really."

"But not you." Hoyt's voice was flat.

"What?" I blinked. "I can fight just as well, maybe better, than most of the citizens you want to get involved."

"I'd like to have you." The regret in his voice sounded genuine, enough for me to overlook his words for a second. Then it hit.

"You'd like to…" It just didn't make sense.

"Kara, you really are slow sometimes," Bani mumbled. "Who do you think runs Bedrock Core?"

I stared at Hoyt. "How old are you?"

He shrugged. "Not sure. Didn't matter - once I stopped growing, I stopped counting. Smaller means it's easier to stay fed."

"And no one pays attention to you if you're a kid," muttered Bani.

I smacked his outstretched leg lightly, and he grinned. We were good again.

But the smile never made it to Hoyt's face. "Sary's got a big reward out for both you and Davien. Too big. You're going to be targeted as long as you're on Neurea until this all dies down."

Well. I stared at nothing until a thump against my leg brought me back. Bani had moved to my other my side. "But I'm going to stay and fight, all right?"

My throat caught, and I couldn't say anything, just wrapped my arm around him in an awkward side-hug. For a moment, he leaned against me, and I thought of all the things he could be, the other futures waiting for him, somewhere else. But he was right, back at the refinery. I hadn't asked him what he wanted.

"You're old enough to decide, kid."

"Honey," a low growl broke through my misery, "what are you doing?"

"I wanted to see your teeth again," Mavi answered, as if it were the most logical answer in the world. Tonight, maybe it was.

Davien cracked one eye, peering up at the girl, who now sat perched on his chest. Apparently, she'd slept enough.

"Mavi, come over here, let him rest," I coaxed. And let him heal, I hoped.

"I'm awake, been mostly awake for a bit." Davien pushed himself up, and Mavi slid into his lap, giggling.

"What's the plan?" The question was to the room in general, but his eyes were fixed on me.

We could stay, I knew. Davien would stay with me, help fight Sary and the rest. All I had to do was say the word.

But I'd promised. And he'd already done his best to make my family safe.

We should go find his.

I snagged the jump bag from the corner where I'd dropped it, and tossed it to him. "See if Rati can break that code."

Hearing her name, Rati rolled into the room. "Of course I can", she snapped, half distracted by Mavi climbing over the front of her chair, happily exploring a new device.

"I can't believe you're doubting my talents after I made you a present."

A helper bot rolled up, carrying a dented gray box.

I took it from the tray, rolled it over in my hand, then looked up at her.

"It was on one of the old mining bots I took over. Didn't take much to separate."

"And it's a..."

She rolled her eyes at me. "You wanted a sensor for antonium, right? Go finish raiding Xavis' storeroom."

My hand clenched around the device, and I laughed. "One last job." I looked at Davien and knew I'd made the right choice. But before we started working... "I've got to get some clean clothes."

~

I'D MEANT to get started early, before the streets were busy, but, by the time we slept, got the kids settled in the new space the bots had prepared, Rati started on the code, and talked over plans with Hoyt and Bani, it was mid-morning.

"You sure you don't want to just get something new?" Davien asked. "I know how much you love shopping."

I poked him in the side, then took his hand. "Save the credits for our tickets. Besides, I want my own, properly broken-in clothes."

"I don't think you'll have anything that fits me," he commented. His pants weren't quite falling off, but close. The jump bag had held only the very, very basics, his datapad, and not much else.

"That's a reasonable expense." I stretched up to kiss his cheek. "Meet you back at my place."

I wedged the door open to the apartment and looked at the chaos I'd left. Running after Davien seemed like a lifetime ago. Certainly, my life had changed.

I stripped down, tossed my coat on the bed and stepped into the refresher, letting the water wash away the stress and terror of the last few days.

Didn't want friends, didn't want entanglements. But I'd had them all along. Maybe not a family of blood, but one of choices.

The refresher beeped, and I cut the water before it turned cold, turning in the jets until I dried.

Rati would make sure I stayed in touch, and I'd threatened

Bani's fingers until he'd promised to work with the littles on the school apps Rati had found. The job would make him keep a unit ahead of them, at least, and keep him out of the worst of the fighting.

I dressed quickly, reveling in clean, untorn clothing. I stretched out on the bed, staring at the ceiling, trying to ignore a soft, persistent beep.

Depending on where the fighting was, another raid on the storeroom would be tricky. If someone else had already taken over the complex, we'd have to count on Rati being eyes and ears for us as we moved in.

Damn it, that sound wasn't going away! Almost as if it were in the room... I stared at my coat, then fumbled through the pockets.

Rati's device was going off. Had been going off, probably the whole time. Great.

I tossed it on top of my dresser. No sense lugging it around if it was broken. The sound increased in both frequency and volume.

That was strange.

I picked it up again, moved it away from the dresser and back again. Maybe some of the dust had gotten on my clothes during the job at Sary's?

I moved it down the front of the dresser, and the noise got louder, only interrupted by Davien forcing open the door.

"I swear, if we stay here another night, I'm moving us back to the Imperial," he grumbled. "What are you doing?"

"Figuring out how broken this thing is," I called back. "We're saving for tickets, remember?"

"Yeah, yeah." He stood beside me, watching as I moved the device up and down. "Kara, what's under there?"

"Nothing," I shrugged. "Just the box..." I trailed off.

He squeezed my hand. "Just the box from your mother?"

I nodded and handed him the device. Kneeling, I pulled the

battered plexi box out from where I'd shoved it so many years ago.

Davien sat on the floor next to me and, as he passed the sensor over the box, it went wild.

"Obviously, it's calibrated to the wrong thing," I mumbled. "Probably whatever she was taking at the end."

"Let's just take a look," Davien said softly, as he put the sensor aside. "Ready?"

I lifted the top and stared into a pile of memories.

A pile of chips. Her papers, her research that she'd moved with us from tiny room to tinier room, unable to let it go.

"Did you ever look through it all?"

"No, it was all from a woman who I didn't know. That woman died, long before she became my mother."

"But what about this?" He lifted a faded print of a woman and child, the child no bigger than Mavi.

"Oh." I took it, ran my finger over the edge of her face. "Mama."

"You look happy," he said, wrapping an arm around my shoulders.

I leaned into him. "I was. I guess I forgot there were good times, too."

Under the print was a fold of pale blue synthisilk. I ran my hand over it, fighting back tears. "My blanket. I refused to sleep without it, for far too long."

I lifted it up, and something clinked into the box, spilling from the folds.

"What...?" I wondered, staring down at the oddly shaped capsules.

Davien picked one up thoughtfully. "Didn't you say she was here to study antonium? Maybe she needed samples for her work."

I stared at the packages, counted, and weighed them in my

mind. "If that's what they are, we don't need to get money for passage off-world..."

He finished my thought. "We can buy our own ship."

I looked again at the print of the woman and child. "She wasn't any older than I am."

"Maybe she was doing the best she could, and got lost along the way."

In the warmth of his touch, I could risk imagining it, how easy it could have been to take that one false step that led to ruin. Maybe she hadn't been ready for such a harsh world, was unprepared to survive on her own. But maybe that wasn't her fault, after all.

Davien's cough pulled me back from my reverie. "This might not be the best time, but honestly, I'm going to bet we don't get a lot of quiet moments."

"What are you doing?"

He twisted to raise up on one knee and pulled a flat rectangular box from behind his back. "I know most women prefer jewelry, but you're not most women." He held the box flat across his palms as if presenting it to me.

Hands trembling, I opened the box. Nestled inside was a knife. Not just a knife, but *my* knife, Untun wood handle gleaming like satin.

I looked at him, shocked to see a trace of uncertainty in his eyes. Not dealing with Xavis, not fighting the Hunter, had he ever looked so vulnerable.

"Stay with me?" he asked softly.

I touched the handle and thought of the night I'd spent looking at the cold, clean stars outside the dome.

Those stars seemed much warmer now.

I took the case from his hands, placed it carefully on the box of memories. Past and future, together.

Then slid into his arms, where I belonged.

"Always," and I kissed him.

Beneath the passion and heat of his kiss, I could taste the sweetness of a promise.

No matter where in the stars we went from here, I would be home with him beside me.

Always.

THE END

CLICK HERE TO READ THE NEXT ADVENTURE!

LETTER FROM ELIN

Dear Reader,

Whoo hooo! Thanks for coming along on this journey with me, Kara and Davien!

This series is a rollercoaster to write, and I hope you're loving the excitement and adventure just as much as the *ahem* steamier bits :)

In the next book, we'll find a little bit more of what happened on the Daedalus, and a few more pieces of the puzzle will slide into place.

If you liked the high stakes and higher passion of Given, you'll love Bonded, because the mystery and intensity are just beginning!

http://myBook.to/StarBreed2

XOXO,

Elin

PREVIEW OF BONDED: STAR BREED
BOOK TWO

Chapter One: Eris

The *Nyx* was never all that fast.

She wasn't the sturdiest or most reputable model on the market, even when she was first built—and I got her second- or third-hand. Some of the repairs I had to figure out to get her to run to my satisfaction drove me up the wall.

Worse, some of them sent me outside her, into the vacuum of space, to work on the outer hull.

No planet-side mechanics for her—she wasn't the kind of ship that was ever meant to land, and after a decade or so of techno-logical advances, most everyone had left models like her behind.

But what the *Nyx* lacked in brawn or speed, she made up for in brains. She was thorough, and curious, and once I'd gotten my hands on her programming and customized everything to my satisfaction, she even had a winning personality.

In our time together, I'd taught her everything I knew, and, together, the two of us made the best damn salvaging team in the Empire.

Well, at least out here in the fringes.

We'd been moving further out the past several years, since most of the asteroid fields in the center of the Empire were pretty well picked-over. As we'd gone further afield, I'd slowly lost contact with everyone I'd known, our messages getting fewer and farther between.

Nixie didn't care—she was a computer, and she had me all to herself.

As far as I was concerned, it was an additional plus. It was already worth it to be off-planet. On *Nyx*, the gravity was much lighter than on planet-side, and I never had to deal with crowds or uncomfortably distant horizons.

"There is no evidence that the wreck has been boarded since shut-down," Nixie said in my ear as I began the sequence to seal up my suit. *"Despite its size, the wreck is hidden effectively from most scanners, as a blip that verifies at roughly 5%. It is also surrounded by other, more noticeable, false positives, both to my scanners and probably also to the naked human eye."*

"Hmm. Sounds like someone wants to hide something." I double-checked the readouts projected onto the visor of my helmet, getting ready to head out into the biggest, darkest unknown. "How long do you think it's been there?"

Nixie paused before answering. *"Unknown. Judging by the ambient temperature of the craft, it has been at least four weeks since the engines have run at standard capacity. It could be as many as six, however."*

"That's a pretty wide margin of error for you," I said, wary.

Most goods worth salvaging didn't come with an expiration date, but the longer a ship had been down, the bigger the chance whatever it had carried would be damaged—or already gone, picked up by someone else.

If Nixie had a nose, she would have sniffed. *"After a certain threshold, cooling is difficult to model, especially in the presence of unknown variables such as—"*

I chuckled. "Okay, girl, I get it. Maybe a month, maybe two?"

"*I may be able to give you a more accurate report once you have completed standard reconnaissance,*" she said, sounding mollified.

"Point taken." Waiting for the air to be drained from the airlock, I double-checked the line I'd be using to abseil over to the ship. "Anything else you can tell me?"

"*Damage to the ship's hull and power systems indicates that she may have been disabled by offensive fire,*" Nixie said over my headset. Her voice was even more metallic than usual in the tiny speakers.

"Attacked, then."

"*It appears so.*"

I whistled silently; that was kind of a mixed bag.

On the one hand, there was sometimes really good freight on ships that had met more violent ends. On the other, there were often much less pleasant leavings, too—the sort of things I'd have nightmares about later.

"Thanks for the warning," I mumbled. Then, before I could lose my nerve, I added, "Fire."

Nixie obliged. I squinted, trying to see the rappel line as it vanished into the distance, but I couldn't be sure it had hit the ship until Nixie gave me the all-clear.

When she did, I triple-checked, as always, to make sure my carabiner was secure. "Keep comms open unless I tell you to take them down, okay? Same goes for main power. And keep an eye out for strangers—ping me if you pick up anything."

"*Understood.*"

I gave Nixie the same orders any time I was away salvaging, but she was a good sport about it, at least. We hadn't had any excitement in a little while, so she was probably enjoying herself at least as much as I was.

"Here I go," I said, and pushed myself through the airlock doors and out into the blackness.

~

Space is big. You can't really say much more than that about it, because when it comes to the scales involved in astronomy as a whole, only understatement can come anywhere close to getting the point across.

Here's another understatement: I've never liked big places. All the planet-dwellers I'd met tended to complain that space stations are too cramped, but even they were big enough to bother me–– and the number of people in them didn't help.

So, the part of my job when I was stuck floating with only a few inches of plastic and metal to separate my body from literally the biggest thing there was? Not my favorite. I dealt with it, though, because the rest of that job was awesome enough to make up for it.

I tried not to think about anything but the ship in front of me, the line I was firing over to it, and how I was going to get the airlock open. Fortunately, most airlocks came with suit-recognition that operated on battery power; it helped minimize accidents, with the added bonus of making my job easier.

Better still, there was enough power that the airlock worked correctly, letting me in, shutting behind me, and filtering air into the room. I moved to take off my helmet.

"You shouldn't do that," Nixie's voice said in my ear. *"Never trust a flotsam ship's systems until you've seen its own diagnostics.' You programmed that into me yourself."*

"Oh, fine, I'll leave it on." I liked tight spaces, sure, but ship's corridors weren't built to accommodate vacuum suits.

It wasn't a model I was familiar with, and I was familiar with most ship models at this point, especially the older ones.

There were signs of damage, too, I noticed as I traversed the hallways. Probably a few serious impacts; the lights were down or flickering in some sections of the hallway, and the temperature regulation system was working irregularly. Whatever had hit this ship had barely left it in one piece.

I narrated my findings to Nixie as I went, and she supplemented my reports with things that the sensors in my suit picked up. Together, we compared the internal damage with the external.

It definitely spelled out a fight that whoever was aboard this ship had lost–badly.

The bridge showed enough signs of damage that I was a little reluctant to set foot in it.

Large windows were usually considered a liability in shipbuilding, but this helm had a window that took up almost an entire wall. There were screens and holographic projection systems everywhere, most of them powered off.

It looked like it was designed to show the ship and its surroundings at every possible angle. The entire setup was more expensive than I'd been expecting, to say the least. It looked a bit like something out of one of the old-fashioned war-drama holos. Except for the lack of bodies. Everyone was long gone.

"Was this thing designed for combat?" I asked Nixie.

"I don't know. I still haven't been able to find a match in my database."

"Hmm." I made my way carefully over to what was probably the captain's chair––it was near the center of the room, and had a large screen attached. "I'll see if there are any logs still in the system."

"If you wanted, I could—"

"No way, girl. You have no idea where this ship's been, you are *not* jacking into it." I unfastened my gloves and searched the side of the screen until I found the wake switch.

Nothing happened.

"All auxiliary power has probably been routed to the life-support systems," Nixie told me.

"Yeah, I was getting there." I stood up and looked around again. There were half a dozen stations around the helm, but the one that I wanted was...

It took me a couple of tries before I figured it out. The screen for the power allocation was the only one to light up right away. "Here we go. Power's being routed to cloaking, even though it's down, so might as well turn that off. Then there's artificial gravity, of course. Life support seems fine..." I trailed off.

"And?" Nixie asked in my ear.

I swallowed. "And suspended animation—two units."

"In use?"

"Seems so." I pulled off my helmet and secured it against the back of my suit, convinced I'd be able to breathe without it. "I guess this ship wasn't quite as abandoned as we thought it was."

I'd never come across live passengers during a salvage before. From what I've heard, it was rare. Passengers on a broken-down ship were usually either rescued immediately, or just plain didn't make it.

And then, of course, most salvagers wouldn't talk much about what they would do if they encountered any. Some of us were more scrupulous than others, and a situation like this started to veer dangerously close to piracy.

Officially, it was my duty to step back now and help any passengers on board. Realistically, not all salvagers did that, and cryo pods were even more of a gray area. Cryogenic pods were expensive, unreliable, and no use if no one ever found them to bring you back.

Most of my peers probably wouldn't judge me too harshly for leaving them as they were and taking everything unessential off the ship. Some probably wouldn't even judge me for switching them off.

Lucky for any possible survivors, it was my call to make rather than someone else's. "Looks like this just turned into a rescue mission," I told Nixie. I double-checked that the power lines to the two pods were secure, made sure I knew how to get there, and then set out.

The pods were located in two different parts of the ship. One was in the medbay, and the other was in an unlabeled room nearer to the engines. The medbay was the closer of the two locations, so I decided to start there.

This part of the ship, too, was different than what I'd been expecting. In any normal ship, the medbay would be pretty small and limited to first-aid and stasis only, but this medbay was large and took almost half a deck.

There were half a dozen small chambers set in the walls, some of them locked with security codes, and an entire wall was lined with cryo pods. All were dark except for one, a tiny green light flashing in the corner.

Normally the thing would've had a screen on the front, providing information about the person inside and about how safe the outside environment was for them. This one didn't have anything like that. Instead, there were two buttons, and one of them was already flush with the surface.

There was something embossed at the top of the pod, too—a number and a name. *G01SN0025 - Med2* . That was all—no window to see into the pod, no customization options, no note of any kind to someone who might come along and discover it.

"What are you seeing?" Nixie asked.

"Not enough to know anything more," I said, and then, "I'm just going to open it."

"Are you sure?" When I didn't answer right away, Nixie pressed on. *"Even if you start the interface, it will still probably take between thirty minutes and several hours for the process of reanimation to be—"*

I pushed the button, and the door launched open in a cloud of steam, almost like it had been spring-loaded. It almost hit me in the face.

I flinched back instinctively, but curiosity drew me back. This wasn't how stasis pods were supposed to behave.

I leaned cautiously in towards the pod, trying to get a good look through the dispersing vapor...

And a large, clawed hand wrapped around my throat.

Click to keep reading - Free in Kindle Unlimited!

http://myBook.to/StarBreed2

NEED TO CATCH UP ON THE STAR BREED?

Don't miss a single one!

Given: Star Breed Book One

When a renegade thief and a genetically enhanced mercenary collide, space gets a whole lot hotter!

Thief Kara Shimsi has learned three lessons well - keep her head down, her fingers light, and her tithes to the syndicate paid on time.

But now a failed heist has earned her a death sentence - a one-way ticket to the toxic Waste outside the dome. Her only chance is a deal with the syndicate's most ruthless enforcer, a wolfish mountain of genetically-modified muscle named Davien.

The thought makes her body tingle with dread-or is it heat?

Mercenary Davien has one focus: do whatever is necessary to get the credits to get off this backwater mining colony and back into space. The last thing he wants is a smart-mouthed thief -

even if she does have the clue he needs to hunt down whoever attacked the floating lab he and his created brothers called home.

Caring is a liability. Desire is a commodity. And love could get you killed.

http://myBook.to/StarBreed1

Bonded: Star Breed Book Two

She doesn't need anyone. He's not going to let her go.

Eris Vance, salvager and loner, is happy with her life in the remote fringes of the Empire with just her AI for company. An abandoned ship could be the find of a lifetime, but it's not nearly as empty as she thinks. And the hulking man left behind kindles a heat she's never felt. But will he stay through the coming storm?

Connor is the perfect soldier - He's been made that way. Waking up to the destruction of the world he knew disturbs him almost as much as the gorgeous woman who found him. Her scent, her touch distracts him, and just this once, maybe he doesn't care.

The *Daedelus* is filled with secrets and the results of genetic experiments to breed the perfect soldier... and now that she's awakened him, the mystery of its destruction will hunt them both. Can the growing bond between them survive?

http://myBook.to/StarBreed2

Caged: Star Breed Book Three

No Past. No Trust. No Way Out.

Zayda Caiden relies on no one. An Imperial spy, her mission was betrayed - but she doesn't know the identity of the traitor.

And there's certainly no reason to trust the giant of a man

dumped at the prison clinic, even if he makes her burn with feelings she thought long buried.

Mack has no memory, no real name. Just dreams of fire and pain, and a set of coordinates to a section of unexplored space he refuses to reveal. There's no room in his mission for a woman with secrets of her own, but her scent fills his dreams.

When they have a chance at freedom, can they trust each other enough to escape? Or will their secrets overwhelm their passion?

http://myBook.to/Starbreed3

Freed: Star Breed Book Four

When solitude leads to the brink of madness, only the touch of a sexy, headstrong doctor can pull a dangerous warrior back from the edge...

Dr. Nadira Tannu's work at the small clinic on Orem station was a quiet practice, helping the people of the Fringe. But then she and one of her patients were abducted into a nightmare on a long lost star ship and nothing would ever be the same.

When a rugged survivor rescues them, can she turn his thirst for revenge into a plan for escape? And can she keep her heart safe from the heat in his eyes?

Vengeance against the faceless droids who destroyed his brothers is all that keeps Ronan alive. But he can't resist the pleading look in a pair of wide green eyes staring at him from a cage.

He'll keep her safe. Even if it's from himself.

http://myBook.to/Starbreed4

Craved: Star Breed Book Five

Compassion. Kindness. Caring.

Not really part of my skill set. But for her, I might have to learn.

Geir

I run advance reconnaissance, collecting intel the Pack needs to execute our operations.

In and out, hard and fast.

And I don't need help.

So when a gorgeous woman saves my life, I'm knocked more than a bit off my game.

That's all it is.

Not the shy smile I hunger to coax from her lips, not the sweet body she keeps hidden. Not the mysteries that haunt her eyes.

And certainly not the bewitching scent that stirs me in ways no mission ever has.

I crave her like nothing I've found before.

Even if she might be the enemy, I'll make her mine.

Valrea

He can't save me.

The secrets of the Compound are too tangled. The nightmares in my blood can never be erased.

But his touch sends me reeling, thirsting for what I can't have.

What harm could one night do?

http://myBook.to/Starbreed5

Snared: Star Breed Book Six

When the only woman Xander cared for was ripped from his arms, nothing else mattered.

Now she's back. Fragile and brave, beautiful and brilliant. Someone to protect, someone to fight for.

Except she doesn't remember him at all.

Her curves and captivating scent drive him mad, demanding he cares for her, possess her.

He'll keep his mate safe, even if the Empire burns to ash around them.

Loree Sarratt is tired of everyone treating her like an invalid. Her hacking skills could save the Empire - if she's not arrested first.

First puzzle to solve? An overprotective pillar of muscle who turns her legs to jelly when he's in the same room.

She can't lose focus. But the heat of his gaze sends her pulse racing. His touch steals her breath. Everything tempts her to surrender...

And forget the danger she's in.

http://myBook.to/Starbreed6

PLEASE DON'T FORGET TO LEAVE A REVIEW!

Readers rely on your opinions, and your review can help others decide on what books they read. Make sure your opinion is heard – http://myBook.to/StarBreed1

If you're interested in keeping up with future releases and opportunities for advance review copies, please join the newsletter!
http://elinwynbooks.com/newsletter/

ABOUT THE AUTHOR

I love old movies – *To Catch a Thief, Notorious, All About Eve* — and anything with Katherine Hepburn in it. Clever, elegant people doing clever, elegant things.

I'm a hopeless romantic.

And I love science fiction and the promise of space.

So it makes perfect sense to me to try to merge all of those loves into a new science fiction world, where dashing heroes and lovely ladies have adventures, get into trouble, and find their true love in the stars!

ALSO BY ELIN WYN

The Empire's Fringe – Science Fiction Romance
The Empire's Fringe Bundle
All of the below stories, at a special price!
https://elinwynbooks.com/the-empires-fringe/
Staked
In the slums of space station Cilurnum 8, fiercely independent Anisha Cheng must decide how far she's willing to trust Kieran Matthias, the one man who she's ever allowed to break her heart. If she can't, she risks losing the Sapphire Star, her late father's bar and the only home she knows, to a crime syndicate in three days. But as Anisha and Kieran try to work together, the plans of the syndicate may break them apart forever.
Jewel of Empire
On the spaceliner Dynomius, reformed cat burglar Audrey Pilgram has three weeks to prove her innocence of a series of copycat crimes, or all the sins of her past will be laid at her door. But her quest to uncover the culprit is complicated when she sees the next target - tall, handsome Phillip Lapsys. Can she stop the theft of the jewel before he steals her heart?
Raven's Heart
Jayna wasn't looking for trouble. Her plan was to keep her head down, save her money, and get back into to med school. But when she overhears the plans for a bio-terrorism attack that could wipe out the population of her station, her world is turned upside down. Raven's Heart is a steamy science fiction romance

complete novella with a happy ending, containing nebula hot scenes of passion.

Stolen

An alien artifact. Archaeologist Eliya Cafeal has spent her life in pursuit of this find - and nothing is going to get in her way. Certainly not a rogue and a scoundrel, even if he makes her blood catch fire. Captain Ruvon Taxal likes his life. Few close friends, a spot of petty smuggling or charter trips as needed. No restrictions, and nothing to tie him down. And if his newest passenger, a feisty archaeologist with storm grey eyes, has gotten under his skin, well, he'll learn to live without her when she leaves. But everything is changed when Eliya is stolen.

Claimed

In the remote mountains of a frontier planet, tinkerer and part-time inventor Paige Roth has her hands full protecting her claim against the goons of MagnorCo. With the help of her robots, she's doing pretty well, but the last thing she expects to fall into one of her traps is a handsome stranger trying to hike through the mountains for reasons of his own. He's handsome enough to make her forget where she put her toolkit, but can she trust him?

ALIEN WARRIOR ROMANCE

https://elinwynbooks.com/alien-romance/

Alien Mercenary's Desire: Alien Abduction Romance

Kordiss has spent his life on the fringe, not succumbing to his rages. But when he rescues feisty human Sharla from intergalactic sex traders, his defenses are breached by her trusting smile. And when she's stolen from his arms, nothing will stand in the way of getting her back.

This is a sexy, steamy stand-alone alien abduction short romance with a happy ending.

Bonded to the Alien: Gate Jumpers Saga Part 1

Captain Taryn Nephalia was, honestly, a little bored with her current mapping mission. But a freak accident sent her and her crew crashing towards an unknown planet. Captured by alien snake men, Taryn knows she's on her own to escape, rescue her crew, and get off that rock.

But she's not expecting help from a fellow prisoner - a hunky alpha alien warrior on mission of his own. And now his mission includes her.

Bonded to the Alien is the first in a linked series of steamy science fiction alien romance short stories about Captain Taryn and her crew.

Allied with the Alien: Gate Jumpers Saga Part 2

Stephine Willovitch isn't sure about trusting the Eiztar warriors. She's practical, logical, and not terribly fond of strangers. As far as she remembered, she'd just entered her pod moments ago. Torpor gas had kept her still for the past 36 hours. But apparently Captain Taryn had gotten them all involved with a bunch of rebels, and now they were on the run from some sort of alien snake men. Stephine would follow orders, but she couldn't be ordered to trust the man paired with her - Dojan Cholsad-. Tall, blond, stunningly handsome - and annoyingly friendly - she certainly wasn't going to put up with any of this bonding nonsense. But when Dojan is in danger, her heart isn't listening to her head.

Trapped with the Alien: Gate Jumpers Saga Part 3

Sherre Balinko, the navigator and youngest of Captain Taryn's crew, couldn't be more excited. She might be stranded on a hostile alien planet, but now they were allied with a whole new group of aliens! Her partner in the race to get the antitoxin back to the base is the tall, handsome Zaddik Wangari. But the grand adventure is over When the Tuvarians board the Eiztar mothership and Sherre and Zaddik must battle them alone...

Lost with the Alien: Gate Jumpers Saga Part 4

Jeline Montias, human pilot, isn't thrilled about being paired with Kogav Wangari of Zurole. He's flippant, grumpy and even though he's an engineer and not a pilot, reluctant to let her at the controls. Why should she care that he has eyes like gorgeous amethyst pools and a sweet smile?

They can't seem to stop arguing, even when they're dodging Tuvarian raiders in their mission to get a deadly poison back to the Eitzar lab for analysis. But when they're driven through a set of jump gates to a new sector, they'll have to work together to survive.

Science Fiction Adventure Romance

Join the men of the Garrison as they discover the secrets of Crucible...

Second Chance at the Stars:

As a gifted psychokinetic healer, Adena Thornwood's skills are in constant demand. She's built a solid reputation for her willingness to make sacrifices at any cost. But when she's betrayed by members of her own family, she may finally be broken. Regaining control will be near impossible with her heart in shambles.

Suppressing the rebellion on Crucible should have been just another mission for Commander Nic Vistuv and the men of his garrison unit. But lies and misinformation plague their mission from the beginning. Ghosts from the past haunt them, threatening his life and those of his brothers-in-arms.

The only way out of their predicament may lie in the form of a bribe, but this bribe is different. It's wrapped in the body of a young healer, whom is battle-scarred and broken by a deep betrayal. As secrets unravel and enemies draw nearer, Adena may be the key to understanding the truth of Crucible.

Can a wounded healer and an embittered soldier come to trust each other in time to forge a second chance for both?

http://elinwynbooks.com/my-books/

Printed in Great Britain
by Amazon